Life of a Good-for-nothing

Life of a
Good-for-nothing

Joseph von Eichendorff

Translated by J. G. Nichols

ET REMOTISSIMA PROPE

100 PAGES

100 PAGES
Published by Hesperus Press Limited
4 Rickett Street, London sw6 1ru
www.hesperuspress.com

First published by Hesperus Press Limited, 2002

English language translation and introduction © J.G. Nichols, 2002

Designed and typeset by Fraser Muggeridge
Printed in the United Arab Emirates by Oriental Press

isbn: 1-84391-004-7

CONTENTS

INTRODUCTION

*If this were played upon a stage now, I could condemn it
as an improbable fiction.*

To imply, as that epigraph does, some resemblance between
Eichendorff's novella and Shakespeare's *Twelfth Night* is not
so far-fetched as might at first seem. Both are set in lands of the
imagination: while Shakespeare's Illyria and Eichendorff's
Germany and Italy can be found on the map, that has little to
do with their reality, or perhaps one should say unreality, in
the fictions. Both works involve a series of apparently random
happenings, where things seldom turn out as people expect,
and yet end, more by luck it would seem than by good
management, with all the pieces of the jigsaw falling neatly, and
happily, into place. Disguise is an important feature of both
works, and even, as a result of the disguise, considerable
confusion over gender. This emphasis on disguise is, of
course, indicative of the way the true course of events is
disguised until the very end. Other details vary. There are no
identical twins in Eichendorff's book, and no Malvolio, no un-
attractive character who remains unreconciled at the end.
Indeed in Eichendorff's more simply sunny work there is no
one of serious ill-intent. The farmer who refuses to direct the
good-for-nothing to Italy and later drives him off his land (a
usual enough procedure with farmers) is the nearest we have
to a villain.

There is even a parallel in Eichendorff's novella to the
epigraph above. By giving one of his characters those words
Shakespeare achieves a comic effect, making the spectator
stand momentarily outside the action and see it clearly as
fiction, and he simultaneously demonstrates with a flourish

that his mastery of his art is such that he can break the spell for an instant while still maintaining the suspension of disbelief. The parallel in Eichendorff is the comment made by one of the company at the musical interlude in Rome when it is disturbed by the irruption of two over-excited young people:

> ' "Barbarian!" shouted one of the men sitting at the round table. "You're rushing right into the middle of an ingenious tableau of the beautiful description by the late lamented E.T.A. Hoffmann, on page 347 of *The Lady's Magazine* for 1816, of Hummel's most beautiful painting which could be seen in the Berlin exhibition in the autumn of 1814!" '

Parallels can be pushed too far, of course. The Never Never Land which Eichendorff creates is, contradictory as it may seem, a distinctly German, and German Romantic, one. Most of the usual stage properties are there: the figure of the wanderer (who likes to set out from a mill), his wanderlust and the homesickness it inevitably brings, his feeling for nature, and the post-horns which, sounding somewhere undefinable in the distance, increase his sense of awe and his wanderlust. These are the features of many familiar *Lieder*. Eichendorff was influenced here, like so many German poets, by the famous collection of folk-songs *Des Knaben Wunderhorn (The Youth's Magic Horn)* of 1805–08, but he was himself also possibly the greatest influence on other writers in the folk-song tradition. If we look for one word to sum up this tradition it is *Sehnsucht* or longing, not longing for anything in particular, just longing. Eichendorff's good-for-nothing travels haphazardly from Germany to Italy and then to Austria, and declares his intention (if that is not too strong a word for one of his temperament) of visiting Italy again after his marriage. In all these travels he is tacitly following the example of Novalis' novel, *Heinrich von Ofterdingen* (1802), whose hero wanders in search of a blue flower once glimpsed in a dream and always afterwards an unattainable ideal.

Two famous German novelists, Theodor Fontane and Thomas Mann, have suggested that the good-for-nothing – this happy-go-lucky, lazy, casual, well-meaning, and rather bumbling creature who throws all the vegetables out of his garden to fill it with flowers – may be seen as the embodiment of the German soul. If only... If only, indeed, any nation could have him as its embodiment! It is more realistic to see him as a walking, or rather sauntering, mockery of certain character-istics often thought of as typical of northern Europeans – philistinism (a word which, in its non-biblical sense, we have taken over from Germany), love of bureaucracy and 'the correct procedures', and the worship of power and success. Without trying to, the good-for-nothing demonstrates the absurdity of the common English notion that a sense of humour is not very German. The book is pervaded by irony, an affectionate irony which shows 'what fools these mortals be' and does it in a pleasant manner. We see this in the way the good-for-nothing respects the learning of the three Prague students because they know a few Latin tags, while they respect him because he is wearing a frock-coat, and all are quite misled. We see it in this passage:

> 'So one Sunday afternoon I was lying in the garden, watching the blue clouds of smoke rising from my pipe, and feeling annoyed that I had not settled into some other occupation which would have at least given me a free Monday to enjoy the next day.'

We see it most of all in the fact that this good-for-nothing, who has no ambition but to follow the whim of the moment, and whose most profound thoughts consist of a string of proverbs, happens to end up being successful.

It is natural to wonder how far this character reflects the author's. On the whole he reflects it like a comic distorting mirror. Unlike our nameless good-for-nothing, Joseph Karl Benedikt Freiherr von Eichendorff was not the son of a miller. He was born into a noble family of Silesia in 1788, in Schloss Lubowitz. Schloss Lubowitz, destroyed towards the end of the Second World War, was a large country mansion, the German word *Schloss* being used, like the French *château*, to refer sometimes to this and sometimes to a fortified castle in the English sense. In the novella the same word is used, therefore, for the palace in which the early events take place, where the good-for-nothing is toll-keeper, and for the forbidding castle in the mountains in Italy. Eichendorff studied law as a young man, but his life was then temporarily overtaken by outside events. His birth had practically coincided with that of the French Revolution. In the subsequent wars the German states were defeated by Napoleon, who even abolished the venerable office of Holy Roman Emperor in 1806. With the destruction of Napoleon's Grand Army in Russia in the winter of 1812, the German states embarked on their famous Wars of Liberation. Eichendorff enlisted first in the Austrian army and then in the Prussian. He never saw any action. By a chance reminiscent of his fiction, his unit arrived on the field of Waterloo on the 19th June 1815, the battle having been fought on the 18th. Most of Eichendorff's working life was then spent in the Prussian civil service, and his spare time in writing. *Life of a Good-for-nothing* appeared, after a long gestation, in 1826. He was a prolific, and extremely skilful, poet. A few years before

Eichendorff's death in 1857, the poet and novelist Theodor Storm described him in a letter: 'He is a gentle and charming person, and much too introspective to have anything about him that might be called distinguished.'

A testimonial written in 1821 to support Eichendorff in obtaining a temporary post in the Prussian civil service is interesting: 'A man of very good reputation and refined, genuinely scholarly, education. He performed his duties very satisfactorily and honourably as a defender of the Fatherland in the recent campaigns. He is a Catholic and performs his religious duties without bigotry or intolerance.' Eichendorff's strong religious faith is clear, implicitly and therefore all the more strongly, throughout his writings, but nowhere more than in this book where the eponymous main character (hero seems hardly the right word, and protagonist sounds much too forceful) is essentially an embodiment of love, and the world he inhabits is clearly conceived in a spirit of love. We are never told his name, and this suggests that his name may be Everyman. If every man is not like him, we do feel while reading this extremely unusual book that things would be better if everyone were like him, although there would then be no one to provide the world with vegetables.

– J. G. Nichols, 2002

ACKNOWLEDGEMENTS

This translation is made from *Aus dem Leben eines Taugenichts*, edited by Hatwig Schultz, Reclam, 2001

Life of a
Good-for-nothing

CHAPTER ONE

My father's mill-wheel was once more rumbling and splashing away, the snow was dripping industriously from the roof, and the sparrows were twittering and playing about. And I was sitting on the doorstep and rubbing the sleep out of my eyes, feeling very comfortable in the warm sunshine. Then my father, who had been bustling about in the mill since daybreak, came out of doors with his nightcap on askew and said to me, 'You good-for-nothing! There you are sunning yourself again and stretching your weary limbs and leaving me to do all the work by myself. I can't go on feeding you any longer. Spring is coming. So out into the wide world with you and earn your own living for once.'

'Right,' I said, 'if I am a good-for-nothing, that's fine, I certainly will go out into the world and seek my fortune.' And in fact I was quite happy with that. It had occurred to me only a short while before to go on my travels, when I heard the yellow-hammer in the treetops, proud and happy once more now that spring had come again, singing, 'Farmer, keep your job!' (Throughout autumn and winter it had been singing outside our windows, 'Hire me, farmer, hire me!') So I went into the house and took off the wall the fiddle I played so well, and my father gave me a few coppers to help me on my way, and off I strolled down the long street and out of the village. I was secretly delighted when to right and left I saw all my old friends and acquaintances going out to work, to dig and plough, as they had done the day before and the day before that and the day before that, while I was free to wander off into the world. In my pride and happiness I called out 'Farewell!' to all the wretched people around, but nobody took much notice. It seemed to me that every day was now a Sunday. And when at last I came out into the open country, I took up my beloved fiddle, and played and sang as I walked along the highway:

To whom God grants his greatest favour
He sends into the wide wide world,
And shows him all his many wonders
In rock, in wood, in stream and field.

The lazybones, who stays home idle,
Is not refreshed when dawn turns red,
But only thinks of cradling children,
Of work and worries, earning bread.

The streams go rushing down the mountains,
The cheerful larks mount up on high,
So why should I not join their chorus
And sing with them full-throatedly?

I shall let God the Father worry
Over maintaining earth and sky.
Who keeps larks, streams, woods, fields so lively
Arranges all that's best for me!

Then I looked round and saw a fine carriage quite close behind me. It must have been coming up for some time without my noticing it, my heart being so full of music, since it was moving very slowly while two noble ladies poked their heads out to listen to me. One was particularly beautiful and much younger than the other, but I liked the look of both of them. When I stopped singing, the elder one had the carriage brought to a halt and said to me kindly, 'Well, young man, you certainly know some lovely songs.'

I answered immediately, 'If your ladyship pleases, I know some much better ones.'

Upon that she asked me, 'Where are you wandering off to at this early hour of the day?'

I am ashamed to say that I did not know myself, so I answered without hesitation, 'To Vienna.' Then they spoke to each other in a foreign language which I did not understand. The younger shook her head several times, but the other was laughing all this time and finally she called out to me, 'Jump up behind. We're going to Vienna too.' No one could have been happier than I was. I made a bow, and with one leap I was on the carriage. The coachman cracked his whip and we flew along the gleaming road, with the wind whistling round my ears.

Below me the village, with its gardens and church towers, was left behind, and in front of me fresh villages, castles and mountains came into view. With fields of grain, bushes and meadows flying past beneath me in all their various colours, and countless larks above me in the clear blue sky, I might have been too bashful to shout out aloud, but within I rejoiced. In fact I jumped and danced about on the footboard so much that I almost dropped my fiddle which I had tucked under my arm. But as the sun rose higher and higher, and heavy white noonday clouds rose up on the horizon all round, and everything in the air and on the broad plain became so empty and still above the gently waving cornfields, then I thought once again of my village and my father and our mill, and how it was so nice and cool in the shade there beside the pond, and how all those things lay so very far behind me. I had the strange feeling that I ought to go back. I put my fiddle between my jacket and waistcoat, settled down thoughtfully on the footboard, and fell asleep.

5

When I opened my eyes the coach was standing still under tall linden trees. Behind them, a broad flight of steps led through pillars into a splendid palace. At one side, through the trees, I could see the towers of Vienna. The ladies seemed to have left long before and the horses had been unhitched. I was very frightened to find myself suddenly so alone, and ran into the palace, hearing laughter from a window above as I did so.

Strange things happened to me in this palace. To begin with, as I was looking round me in the wide cool entrance hall, someone tapped me on the shoulder with a stick. I turned round quickly and saw a tall man in state dress. He had a broad sash of gold and silk hanging down to his hips, he was holding a staff with a silver knob on the end, and there was an extraordinarily long, hooked, princely nose on his face. Large and splendid, like a puffed-up turkeycock, he asked me what I was doing there. I was quite dumbfounded, what with fright and astonishment, and could not find anything to say. Then several servants came running along from above and below. They said nothing, but simply looked me up and down. Then a chambermaid – as I learned later – came straight up to me and said I seemed like a nice fellow and that her mistress wished to know if I would like to serve there as a gardener's boy. I felt in my waistcoat, but my few coppers were no longer there. Who knows? They must have fallen out of my pocket while I was dancing about on the coach. I had nothing left but my fiddle, and the man with the staff had said as he went by that he would not have given a farthing for that. So in fear and trembling I told the chambermaid that I would like the job, looking sideways at the sinister figure which, moving back and forth in the hall like the pendulum of a clock in a tower, was just emerging once more majestically and frighteningly out of the background. Finally the gardener came, muttered something under his breath about rogues and bumpkins, and led me into the garden, giving me a long sermon as we went. I must be sober and hardworking, not wander about in the world, and not engage in unprofitable arts and useless nonsense. In this way I might, with time, amount to something. There were several other very fine, well-composed, useful pieces of advice, but I have since forgotten almost all of them. Anyway I really did not know how it had all come about, and I simply went on saying yes to everything. I was like a bird that has just been drenched in water. At any rate I did now, thank heaven, have a living.

Life was pleasant in the gardens. Every day I had plenty to eat and more money than I needed to buy wine. The only thing was that unfortunately I had a lot of work to do. I liked the temples, arbours and beautiful green avenues very much. If only I had been able to stroll through them peacefully and carry on a sensible conversation, like the gentlemen and ladies who came there every day! Whenever the gardener was away and I was left alone, I would take out my short pipe, settle down, and devise fine precious phrases with which to entertain the beautiful young lady who had brought me to the palace, had I been a nobleman sauntering round with her. On sultry afternoons, when everything was so still that only the buzzing of the bees could be heard, I would lie on my back and watch the clouds flying over me towards my village and the grasses and flowers swaying to and fro, and think about the beautiful lady. Then it often happened that she would pass through the gardens in the distance with a guitar or a book, as calm and friendly as the vision of an angel, so that I did not really know whether I was dreaming or awake.

Once, as I was passing by a summer-house on my way to work, I sang to myself:

Wherever I may wander,
Through valley, wood, and field,
From mountain top to meadow,
I, lovely gracious lady,
Greet you a thousandfold.

Then, from inside the cool dark summer-house and between the half-opened blinds and the flowers, I saw two young sparkling eyes flash out. I was so amazed that I did not finish the song, but went off to work without one look back.

One Saturday, in the evening, I was standing at the window of the gardener's house, enjoying the prospect of Sunday and still thinking of the sparkling eyes, when suddenly the chambermaid came wandering along through the twilight. 'My mistress sends you this so that you may drink her health. Goodnight to you!' At that she put a bottle of wine quickly onto the window-ledge and disappeared among the flowers and hedges like a lizard.

But I stood there for a long time in front of that marvellous bottle and could hardly believe what had happened to me. And if I was accustomed to playing my fiddle well enough, now I played and sang as never before. I sang the whole of the song of the beautiful lady and all the songs I knew, until outside all the nightingales were awake and the moon and stars had been standing for a long time over the gardens. Yes, that was a really beautiful night!

No one knows what Fate has in store. Every dog has his day. He who laughs last laughs longest. The age of miracles is not over. Man proposes, God disposes. So I pondered on the days following as I sat once more in the garden with my pipe; and it seemed to me, as I considered myself carefully, that I really was a bit of a wastrel. In contrast with my previous habit I now rose very early every day, before the gardener and the other workers were stirring. It was so wonderful outside in the gardens. The flowers, the fountains, the rose bushes and the whole garden sparkled like pure gold and jewels in the morning sun. And in the avenues of high beeches it was as calm, cool and solemn as a church. Only the birds were fluttering and pecking at the sand. Immediately in front of the palace, just below the windows where the beautiful lady lived, was a flowering bush. I went there every day at earliest morning and hid behind the branches in order to gaze at the windows, for I lacked the courage to show myself in the open. Every day I saw the beautiful lady, still warm and half asleep in her snow-white dress, come to the open window. Then she would plait her dark brown hair and let her charming playful eyes wander over my bush and the garden, and then she would tie up the flowers which stood in front of her window, or even take her guitar in her white arms and sing to its accompaniment so wonderfully across the garden that I still feel melancholy clutching my heart whenever I recall those songs. But all that was so long ago!

This lasted about a week. But on one occasion, while she was standing once more right by the window and everything was quiet all round, a fatal fly flew into my nose and I started sneezing loudly and could not stop. She leaned far out of the window and saw me, wretch that I was, lurking behind the bush. So I was ashamed and for many days I stayed away.

Eventually I did dare to go there once again. But this time the window was shut and, although I sat behind the bush for four, five, six days, she did not come to the window any more. Then I became tired of waiting, so I took my courage in both hands and every morning I went openly round the palace under all the windows. But the beautiful beloved lady did not appear. A little further on I always saw the other lady standing at her window. I had never looked at her so closely before. She was fine, red and plump, and quite magnificent and haughty in appearance, like a tulip. I always made her a deep bow, and I cannot deny that she thanked me every time and nodded and at the same time her eyes sparkled remarkably courteously. Only on one occasion did I think I saw my beautiful lady standing behind the curtain and peeping out stealthily.

Many days went by without my seeing her. She came into the gardens no more; she came to the window no more. The gardener scolded me for my laziness, and I was discontented, and the tip of my own nose seemed to get in the way when I looked out upon God's wide world.

So one Sunday afternoon I was lying in the garden, watching the blue clouds of smoke rising from my pipe, and feeling annoyed that I had not settled into some other occupation which would have at least given me a free Monday to enjoy the next day. The other lads meanwhile had put on their best clothes and gone off to the dance-halls in the suburbs nearby. There the people were all swarming and surging back and forth in the warm air in their Sunday best, among the gleaming houses and the barrel organs. But I was sitting like a bittern in the reeds of a lonely pool in the garden, rocking myself in the boat that was moored there, while the evening bells were ringing out from the city, and the swans were slowly moving back and forth beside me on the water. I felt like death.

Then I heard in the distance a confusion of voices, a lot of happy talk and laughter, which came nearer and nearer. Then red and white shawls, hats and feathers glimmered through the greenery, and all at once a crowd of brightly dressed young people came from the palace across the meadow towards me with my two ladies among them. I stood up and tried to get away, but the elder of the ladies saw me. 'Oh, there's an answer to a prayer,' she cried out to me with a laugh. 'Row us to the other side of the lake!' One after another the ladies stepped cautiously and fearfully into the boat. The gentlemen helped them and boasted a little of their own bravery on the water. When the ladies had all settled on the benches at the sides of the boat, I pushed off. One of the young gentlemen, who was standing near the prow, began to rock almost imperceptibly. Then the ladies looked about them in their fear and some of them even screamed. My beautiful lady, who was holding a lily in her hand, sat close to the side of the boat and looked down into the clear waves as she touched them with her lily, smiling quietly as she did so, so that her whole image was visible in the water among the reflected clouds and trees, like an angel moving gently through the deep blue space of heaven.

While I was gazing at her, it suddenly occurred to the other lady, the plump happy one, that I should sing something during the trip. A very elegant young gentleman with spectacles on his nose, who was sitting by her, turned towards her quickly, kissed her hand gently and said, 'What a clever idea! A folk-song, sung by the people themselves in the open fields and woods, is like an Alpine rose which is actually growing on the Alps. It is the soul of our nation, while *Magic Horns*[1] are mere collections of dried plants.' But I said I had nothing to sing which was worthy of such a noble company.

Then the pert chambermaid, who was standing near me with a basket full of glasses and bottles and whom I had not noticed before, said, 'But you do know a very pretty song about a very lovely lady.'

'Yes, yes, sing that, and sing away,' cried the plump lady.

I went red all over. Then the beautiful lady looked up suddenly from the water and looked at me and her look went right through me. Without more ado, I took heart and sang out of the fullness of my joy:

Wherever I may wander,
Through valley, wood, and field,
From mountain top to meadow,
I, lovely gracious lady,
Greet you a thousandfold.

I seek out in my garden
Such flowers, white, red, and blue,
And with them I weave garlands
And bind my thoughts together
And greetings with them too.

I cannot give a garland
To her, so high and fine,
So they will have to perish.
But love that has no equal
Must in my heart remain.

I seem to be so happy,
Pretending to be brave,
And as my heart is breaking,
I'm digging as I'm singing,
And digging my own grave.

We came to land and the company disembarked. I had noticed that, while I was singing, many of the young men were making fun of me to the ladies with sly looks and whispers. The bespectacled gentleman shook my hand as he went away and said something, I cannot remember what, and the elder of my ladies gave me a very friendly glance. My beautiful lady had held her eyes down throughout my song and now she went away without saying a word. As for me, the tears stood in my eyes while I was singing, and my heart seemed about to break for shame and anguish at the song. I realised then, all at once, how beautiful she was, and how poor I was and how scorned and forsaken by the whole world. And when they had all disappeared behind the bushes, I could not restrain myself any longer. I threw myself down on the grass and wept bitterly.

CHAPTER TWO

Close to the gardens, and separated from them only by a high wall, ran the highway. By the side of it a neat little toll-house with a red-tiled roof had been built, behind which was a little flower garden, with a painted fence round it, that through a gap in the wall gave onto the most shady and hidden part of the palace gardens. The toll-keeper who used to live there had recently died. One morning very early, when I was still lying in a deep sleep, the palace secretary came to me and summoned me straightaway to the steward. I dressed rapidly and strolled along behind the happy-go-lucky secretary who as he went picked the occasional flower to pin on his jacket and fenced skilfully in the air with his walking stick and made various remarks to me over his shoulder, none of which I understood because my eyes and ears were still full of sleep. When I entered the office, where day had not yet quite dawned, the steward looked at me from behind a monstrous ink-well and piles of papers and books and an imposing wig, like an owl looking out of its nest, and said, 'What is your name? Where do you come from? Can you write, read and count?' When I said yes, he went on, 'Well then, in consideration of your good conduct and extraordinarily good manners, her ladyship wishes you to fill the vacant post of toll-keeper.' Quickly I considered my previous conduct and manners, and in the end even I had to admit that the steward was right. And so, before I knew it, I became a genuine toll-keeper.

I took possession of my new dwelling and in no time at all I had settled in. I found one or two useful things which the late lamented collector had bequeathed to his successor, among them a splendid red dressing-gown with yellow spots, a pair of green slippers, a nightcap and some pipes with long stems.

They were just what I had desired while I still lived at home, where our village priest used to get along nicely with such things. So I spent the whole day (there were no further duties to perform) sitting on the bench in front of my house in dressing-gown and nightcap, smoking the longest pipe I could find amongst the late lamented collector's bequest, and watching the people walking, driving and riding to and fro on the highway. I only wished that for once a few people from my village, who always said that I would never amount to anything in my whole life, could pass by and see me like this. The dressing-gown suited me very well and all in all I was very nicely placed. So I sat there and thought of this and that, how everything was difficult to begin with, and how the aristocratic life was a very comfortable one, and I made a formal decision to give up all this travelling from now on and to save up money as other people did and eventually make something of myself in the world. Meanwhile, despite my decisions, worries, and duties, I by no means forgot about the beautiful lady.

I tore up and threw away all the potatoes and other vegetables which I found in my garden, and replanted it entirely with only the choicest flowers. At this the major-domo with the large princely nose, who since I lived there visited me often and had become my close friend, looked at me askance with some apprehension, and thought I must be someone whose good luck had sent him off his head. But that was nothing to me. For not far off, in the palace gardens, I had heard the sound of gentle voices, among which I thought I recognised that of my beautiful lady, although the dense bushes prevented my seeing anyone. So every day I made a bouquet of the most beautiful flowers I had, climbed over the wall each evening once it was dark, and put the bouquet on a stone table which stood in the middle of an arbour. And every evening, when I brought the new bouquet, the old one had gone from the table.

One evening the company had gone out hunting. The sun was just going down and covering the whole landscape with a glow and a glimmer; the Danube, all gold and fire, was winding away into the distance, and on every hillside the vine-dressers were singing away. I was sitting with the major-domo on the bench in front of my house, savouring the mildness of the air as the pleasant day was slowly darkening and its last sounds dying out. Suddenly the horns of the returning hunters could be heard in the distance, echoing each other from time to time among the hills. This gave me enormous pleasure and I leapt up and cried out in my rapture, 'Now that's what I call a noble occupation – hunting!'

But the major-domo quietly knocked his pipe out and said, 'That is what *you* think. I've tried it. You earn scarcely enough to pay for the shoes you wear out, and you're never free of coughs and colds, which comes from having your feet wet all the time.' I hardly know why, but I was overcome by a sense-less rage so that my whole body literally shook. Suddenly I found everything about the man – his tedious cloak, his ever-lastingly wet feet, his snuff, his huge nose – utterly detestable.

Almost beside myself, I grabbed him by the coat and said, 'Major-domo, clear off back home, or I'll give you a good thump!' This confirmed him in his old opinion that I was crazy. He looked at me thoughtfully and rather fearfully, left without a word and, looking back uneasily from time to time, strode off to the palace, where he declared breathlessly that I had gone raving mad.

But in the end I had to laugh about it. In fact I was glad to be free of my friend with all his great wisdom, for by now it was time for me to put my bouquet in the arbour. So I leapt over the wall and was going towards the stone table when I heard a horse's hooves in the distance. I could not escape. It was my beautiful gracious lady herself. She was already here, in green hunting dress with feathers nodding on her hat, riding slowly as though lost in thought along the avenue towards me. I felt that it was just like the story of the beautiful Magelone which I had read long ago in my father's old books, as she came along with the sound of the horns drawing nearer all the time in the changing evening light. I was rooted to the spot. But when she became aware of me she gave a sudden start, and almost pulled her horse up involuntarily. I was nearly beside myself, my heart throbbing with apprehension and in extremity of joy. When I noticed that she was indeed wearing my bouquet of yesterday on her breast, I could no longer contain myself but said in all my confusion, 'Gracious lady, take this bouquet also from me, and take all the flowers which grow in my garden, and everything I have! I would go through fire and water for you!' She had been gazing at me earnestly, almost as though she were annoyed, with a look that went right through me. But now, while I was speaking, she kept her eyes down. Just then the sound of riders and their voices could be heard from the bushes. She snatched the bouquet out of my hand and soon, without saying a word, she had disappeared at the end of the arcade.

From that evening I knew no peace of mind. I felt all the time, as I used to at home at the beginning of spring, restless and happy without knowing why, as if some great stroke of luck awaited me, or at least something extraordinary. In particular, I could not manage the abominable bookkeeping at all. When the gold and green light of the sun shone through the chestnut tree outside the window and fell onto the figures, and went up and down nimbly adding up the sums brought

17

forward and the sum-totals, I was so lost in such strange thoughts that I often became completely confused and truly could not even count up to three. For 8 always looked to me like my plump, tightly laced lady with the large headdress, and the evil 7 was just like a signpost always pointing back, or a gallows. The funniest was 9 which, before I knew where I was, stood on its head and became a 6. Meanwhile 2, like a question mark, looked at all this knowingly as if to say to me, 'What will become of you in the end, you wretched o? Without her, this slender 1, you will always be simply nothing.'

It was no longer a pleasure to sit out of doors. To make myself rather more comfortable, I took out a footstool and put my feet on it, and I patched an old parasol which had belonged to the toll-keeper and held it over myself like a Chinese pavilion to shade me from the sun. But nothing helped. It seemed to me, as I sat there and smoked and meditated, that my legs were growing gradually longer out of boredom, and my nose was growing larger as I did nothing but look down on it hour after hour. Often before daybreak a special mail-coach would come by and I would go out into the fresh air half asleep, and a pretty little face, of which only two sparkling eyes could be seen in the half-light, would look out of the coach in curiosity and give me a friendly good morning, while in the villages round about cocks were crowing briskly across the rippling cornfields, and through the streaks of dawn high in the heavens some early risers among the larks were already soaring. Then the coachman would take his horn and drive on, blowing and blowing all the while. And then I would stand there for a long time, gazing after the coach and feeling that I ought to go away immediately out into the wide wide world.

Meanwhile I went on laying my bouquets as soon as the sun

had set on the stone table in the shady arbour. But it was all over now since that evening. Nobody bothered with it any longer. Whenever I went to look in the early morning, the flowers lay there as they had lain the day before, and looked really sad with their withered heads hanging down and drenched with drops of dew, as though they were weeping. This annoyed me. I made no more bouquets. In my garden the weeds might spread as much as they liked, and I let the flowers grow until the wind blew their petals away. It was just as wild and colourful and confused in my heart.

During this critical period it happened once, while I was lying at the window inside my house and looking out disconsolately into the empty air, that the chambermaid came tripping along across the road from the palace. She turned quickly when she saw me and came and stood by the window. 'The master returned from his travels yesterday,' she said hurriedly.

'And so?' I asked in some surprise. (For several weeks now I had not bothered with anything at all and did not even know that the master had gone on his travels.) Then I said, 'Well, his daughter, the gracious young lady, must have been very pleased at that.'

The chambermaid looked me up and down so strangely that I really began to wonder if I had said something stupid. 'You know nothing at all,' she said eventually and wrinkled up her little nose. 'Well now,' she went on, 'this evening there is to be a dance and masquerade in the palace in the master's honour. My lady will go disguised as a flower-girl. You understand, as a flower-girl? Now my lady has noticed that you have some particularly beautiful flowers in your garden.' I thought to myself how strange it was that by now the flowers could hardly be seen for weeds. However, she went on, 'My lady wants some flowers for her dress. But she wants them completely fresh, straight from the garden, so you must bring them this evening when it is dark and wait under the big pear tree in the palace gardens until she comes to fetch them.'

I was flabbergasted by this news and in my rapture I left the window and ran outside.

'Ugh, what a horrible dressing-gown!' she cried out when she saw me in all my finery. That annoyed me, but I did not want to be behindhand in gallantry, so I capered about a bit, rather skilfully, and made as if to catch her and kiss her. Unfortunately, however, the dressing-gown, which was much too long for me, got caught in my feet and I measured my length on the ground. When I had pulled myself together the chambermaid was already far off, and I heard her laughing in the distance. She must have been holding her sides with laughter.

But now I had something to think about and to be pleased about. So she was still thinking of me and my flowers! I went into my garden and quickly pulled all the weeds out and threw them up high above my head into the gleaming air, as though I were rooting out all evil and melancholy at the same time. The roses reminded me once more of her mouth, the azure morning glories reminded me of her eyes, and the snow-white lilies with their sad, drooping heads looked just like her too. I put them all together carefully into a little basket. It was a calm and beautiful evening and there was not a cloud in the sky. A few isolated stars were already visible, the Danube could be heard rippling in the distance across the fields, and in the high trees in the palace gardens nearby countless birds were singing in chorus to me. Oh, how happy I was!

When at last it was dark, I took my basket and set off for the palace gardens. Everything in the basket was so colourful and charmingly mixed, white, red, blue, and scented, that my heart leapt up when I looked inside.

Full of good cheer, I went by the light of the moon along the quiet pathways all carefully strewn with sand, over the small white bridges beneath which the swans were asleep on the water, and on past the splendid arbours and summer-houses. I found the big pear tree very easily, for it was the very same one I used to lie under on the hot afternoons when I was still the gardener's boy.

It was so dark and lonely there. Only one tall aspen was trembling and murmuring in its silver leaves. Now and again the sound of dance music rang out from the palace. I could hear people's voices too at times in the gardens. Often they came quite near to me, then it all grew suddenly quiet again.

My heart was throbbing. I had an uncanny feeling as though I were about to rob someone. For a long time I stood stock-still, leaning on the tree and listening. But when no one came I could bear it no longer. I hung my basket on my arm and climbed up quickly into the tree, just to breathe fresh air once more.

Up there the sound of the dance music came to me more clearly than ever across the tops of the trees. I could overlook the whole garden and even see into the brightly lit windows of the palace. There the chandeliers were turning slowly like garlands of stars, innumerable ladies and gentlemen in all their finery were undulating and waltzing, mingling like the figures in a shadow-play, some of them sometimes coming to the window to look out into the garden. Outside the palace, the lawn, the bushes and the trees shone like gold in the light from the ballroom, so that it seemed the birds and flowers must awaken. But all around me and far away behind me the gardens were dark and silent.

So there I was all by myself up in the tree. 'Well, she is dancing now,' I thought, 'and must have forgotten you and your flowers a long time ago. They are all very happy and no one's bothering about you. Indeed, such has always been my fate. Everyone else has his appointed place, his own warm stove, his cup of coffee, his wife, his glass of wine in the evening, and is thoroughly content. Even the footman is quite happy with his lot. But I always seem to be a latecomer, arriving when nobody expects me anymore.'

While I was philosophising in this way, I suddenly heard a rustling down in the grass. Two genteel voices were talking softly together, quite nearby. Then the branches in the shrubbery parted, and the chambermaid poked her face out of the foliage and looked about on all sides. The moonlight sparkled on her cunning eyes as she peeped out. I held my breath and stared down. It was not long before the flower-girl stepped out from among the trees, just as the chambermaid had told me yesterday she would. My heart was throbbing madly. But she was wearing a mask and appeared to be looking round in astonishment. Then I had the feeling that she was not as slender and dainty as I remembered her. At last she came quite near to the tree and took off her mask. It was in fact the other, older lady!

You can imagine how glad I was, after I had recovered from the initial shock, to be up there in safety. How in the world did *she* come to be here just at this time? Suppose my beautiful beloved lady came now to get the flowers? That would be a fine how-d'ye-do! I was ready to burst into tears out of sheer vexation.

Meanwhile the would-be flower-girl said, 'It's so stifling up in the ballroom that I had to walk about in the open air just to cool down.' As she said this she was fanning herself all the time with her mask and puffing and panting. In the bright moonlight I could clearly see how the sinews in her neck stood out. She was very angry and as red as a beetroot. The chambermaid was searching round all the hedges as though she had lost a needle.

'I really must have some flowers if I'm to play my part properly,' the flower-girl went on. 'Where can he have got to?' The chambermaid went on searching and sniggering to herself. 'Did you say something, Rosette?' demanded the flower-girl sharply.

'I'm saying what I've always said,' replied the chambermaid, putting on an earnest and guileless face. 'The toll-keeper is a complete lout and always will be. I've no doubt he's lying asleep somewhere behind a bush.'

I was itching to jump down and salvage my reputation, but just then among the general noise and music the sound of a kettledrum could be heard from the palace.

Now the flower-girl could contain herself no longer. 'They are cheering the master now,' she said in her vexation. 'Come on! We'll be missed.' And with that she replaced her mask and rushed back in a rage to the palace with the chambermaid. The trees and bushes in some strange way seemed to point after her with their long noses and fingers, and the moonlight danced nimbly up and down her broad figure, as on a keyboard. And so she made her exit, like a singer from the stage, to the sound of trumpets and drums.

But up in my tree I hardly knew what was going on, and I turned my eyes to stare at the palace. A group of high torches down on the steps of the entrance cast a strange light on the gleaming windows and far out into the gardens. It was the servants who were serenading their young master. In the middle of them stood the major-domo, all dressed-up like a minister of state, in front of a music stand, working away diligently on a bassoon.

I was just settling down to listen to this beautiful serenade, when the folding doors on the palace balcony flew open. A tall gentleman, handsome and distinguished, dressed in uniform with many glittering decorations, walked out onto the balcony. He led my beautiful young lady by the hand. She was all in white, like a lily in the dark, or like the moon moving over a clear night sky.

I could not turn my eyes away, and gardens, trees and lawns disappeared from my sight; she looked so wonderful standing there, tall and slender, in the light of the torches, speaking charmingly to the handsome officer, or nodding in a friendly way to the musicians below. The people down there were beside themselves with joy, and finally I could restrain myself no longer and I bellowed out, 'Hurrah!' with all the others.

However, when they had eventually left the balcony, and the torches below had been extinguished one by one, and the music stands had been taken away, and all the gardens were dark again and rustling as they had before – then I realised for the first time with a sinking feeling that it was really only the aunt who had wanted me to bring flowers, that my beautiful lady did not think of me at all and had long been married, and that I myself was a complete idiot.

All that plunged me into an abyss of meditation. I shrank back, like a hedgehog, inside the prickles of my own thoughts. From the palace the dance music came less and less frequently. The lonely clouds drifted away over the dark gardens. And so, with the ruin of all my hopes, I sat there up in the tree throughout the hours of darkness like a night-owl.

Eventually the cold morning air wakened me from my dreams. I was truly amazed once I started to look about me.

The dancing and music had stopped long since, and the palace and the lawns and the stone steps and pillars looked so calm, cool and solemn. Only the fountain in front of the entrance went on with its lonely splashing. Here and there in the branches around me the birds were already waking, ruffling their coloured feathers and stretching their wings and gazing curiously at their unexpected bedfellow. The sun's bright rays sparkled on my breast and away across the gardens.

I sat up in my tree and for the first time in ages looked far into the distance, to where a few boats were already making their way along the Danube between the vineyards on the hills, and to where the still empty roads stretched like bridges across the gleaming countryside and over hills and valleys.

I don't know why, but suddenly I was once again in the grip of my former wanderlust, with all its old sadness and joy and expectations. And in that same instant I thought of how my beautiful lady was sleeping in the palace between silk sheets and surrounded by flowers, with an angel sitting by her bed in the morning hush. 'No,' I cried out aloud, 'I must get away from here, further and further away, wherever the sky is blue above me!'

Therewith I flung my basket high into the air. It was wonderful to see the flowers falling through the branches to come to rest in all their different colours on the lawn beneath. Then I too went down quickly and through the silent gardens to my house. I did occasionally pause at places where I had once seen her or had thought about her as I lay in the shade. .

Inside and outside my little house everything looked as it did when I left it the day before. The garden lay waste after my plundering, the big book of accounts was open in my room, and my fiddle, which I had almost forgotten, hung on the wall, covered with dust. But just at that moment a ray of sunshine came through the window opposite and flashed upon the strings. That found an echo in my heart. 'Yes,' I said, 'you must come with me, you faithful instrument! Our kingdom is not of this world!'

And so I lifted my fiddle from the wall, left the ledger, the dressing-gown, the slippers, the pipes and the parasol where they were, and wandered out of my house as poor as when I had come into it, and found myself outside on the gleaming highway.

I looked back very often. I felt strange, very sad and yet very happy once more, like a bird escaped from its cage. And when I had already gone quite a way, I took up my fiddle and sang in the open air:

> *I shall let God the Father worry*
> *Over maintaining earth and sky.*
> *Who keeps larks, streams, woods, fields so lively*
> *Arranges all that's best for me!*

The palace with its gardens and the towers of Vienna had already disappeared behind me into the morning haze, and innumerable larks were singing joyfully high in the sky above me as I walked between the green hills and through cheerful towns and villages down towards Italy.

CHAPTER THREE

But there was one fly in the ointment! It had not occurred to me that I did not know the way, and at that hour of the morning there was no one around for me to ask, while ahead of me the highway divided into several new roads stretching far away over the highest mountains. They seemed to be leading right out of the world, so that I felt dizzy just to look at them.

At last a farmer came along, who I thought must be going to church, since it was a Sunday. He wore an old-fashioned coat with big silver buttons and carried a big bamboo walking-stick with a huge silver knob on it that shone from a long way off in the sunshine. I asked him very politely, 'Can you tell me the way to Italy?' The farmer stopped, looked at me, thought for a while with his lower lip sticking out a long way, and then looked at me again. I said once more, 'To Italy, where they grow oranges?' 'What have your oranges got to do with me?' said the farmer, and strode off. I had expected better of him, for he looked very distinguished.

Now what could I do? Turn round and go back to my village? Then people would have pointed at me, and the children would have jumped about around me, saying, 'Welcome back from the world! Well, what's it like in the world? Did you bring any gingerbread back from the world?' The major-domo with the princely nose, who was very knowledgeable in the geography of the world, had often said to me, 'Worthy and esteemed toll-keeper, Italy is a beautiful country, where the good God looks after everything. You can lie on your back in the sunshine there and the raisins fall into your gob, and if a tarantula bites you, you dance about with uncommon agility, even if you never learned to dance.' 'Well then, Italy it is, Italy!' I shouted out loud, and without thinking about the different ways I ran down the first road I came to.

When I had wandered along for some distance, I saw on the right a lovely orchard where the morning sunlight was shining so brightly through the trunks and treetops that the grass seemed to be covered with a golden carpet. Since I could see no one about I climbed over the low fence and lay down comfortably in the grass, for my limbs were still aching from the previous night's lodging in the tree. You could see all the country round from there, and because it was Sunday the sound of church-bells could be heard coming from far away across the silent fields, and country people in their Sunday best were making their way past meadows and bushes to church. I felt quite at ease, the birds were singing in the trees above me, I thought about my mill and my beautiful lady's gardens, and how everything was now so very far away – until finally I fell asleep.

Then I dreamt that my beautiful lady came walking towards me, or rather floating down to me, out of the glorious country-side, amid the sound of the church-bells, veiled all in white, her long dress fluttering in the red light of dawn. And then the next moment it seemed that we were not in foreign parts but in my village by the mill in the deep shade. Then everything was quiet and deserted, as it is on Sunday when people are in church and only the sound of the organ comes through the trees, and I was really sick at heart. But my beautiful lady was very kind and friendly, she held me by the hand and went with me, and as we walked together in that solitude she sang the lovely song she used to sing in the early morning to her guitar at the open window. And as she did so I saw her reflection in the calm lake, a thousand times more beautiful, but with strange large eyes staring at me so fixedly that I was almost afraid. Then all at once the mill started up, at first with slow deliberate movements, then roaring faster and faster and more and more violently. The lake darkened and its water was disturbed. My beautiful lady turned quite pale, and her veils became longer and longer and fluttered horribly in streamers, like streaks of mist high in the heavens. The sound of the mill-wheel grew louder and louder, while the major-domo seemed to be blowing on his bassoon, until at last with my heart throbbing violently I awakened.

A wind really had arisen, coming to me gently through the branches overhead. But what was roaring and blustering was neither the mill nor the major-domo, but that very farmer who previously had not wished to show me the way to Italy. He had taken off his Sunday clothes and stood in front of me in his white shirtsleeves. 'Well,' he said, while I was still rubbing the sleep from my eyes, 'I suppose you're hoping to pick some oranges here, while you trample down all the nice grass, you lazy lout!'

I was annoyed that the ruffian had wakened me. I jumped up angrily and retorted, 'Who are you to tell me off? I have been a gardener, before you knew anything about it, and a toll-keeper, and if you had been there you would have had to raise your dirty cap to me. And I had my own house and a red dressing-gown with yellow spots.' But the clodhopper was not interested in any of that. He simply put both hands on his hips and said, 'What do you want, eh?' While he was speaking I realised that he was, to tell you the truth, a short, sturdy, bandy-legged fellow with bulging, staring eyes and a red, somewhat crooked nose. And as he said nothing but 'Eh! Eh!', taking a step nearer to me every time he said it, I suddenly had a strange sense of dread. I jumped up quickly, leapt over the fence and, without looking back once, I ran across the fields, with my fiddle twanging in my pocket.

When at last I paused to draw breath, the garden and valley were no more to be seen, and I found myself standing in a beautiful wood. But I did not pay much attention to that, for I found the whole business more infuriating than ever, particularly the fellow's lack of politeness. So for quite a while I stood there telling him off to myself.

With such thoughts in mind I walked on rapidly, and got further and further from the highway and closer to the mountains. I was in a blind alley. When it came to a sudden end, I found that in front of me there was only a narrow little-used footpath. There was no one to be seen all round and no sound could be heard. All the same it was pleasant walking there, with the treetops rustling and the birds singing. So I put myself in God's hands, took out my fiddle, and played all my favourite pieces until the lonely wood re-echoed with the sound.

But the playing did not last long, for I kept on falling over the blessed roots of the trees, and I started to get hungry too, while there seemed to be no end to the wood. So I wandered around the whole day, with the sun slanting through the trees, until at last I came out into a little green valley surrounded by mountains and full of red and yellow flowers with countless butterflies fluttering round them in the golden sunset. It was so lonely there that the world seemed to be a hundred miles away. Except for the chirping of the crickets, the only sound came from a shepherd who was lying down in the long grass and playing so mournfully on his reed pipe that it was quite heartbreaking. 'Yes,' I thought, 'how nice to be an idler like that, while people like me have to fight for their living and keep their wits about them!' A clear little stream, which I could not cross, flowed between us. So I called out to him and asked where the nearest village was. He did not stir himself except to raise his head slightly and point with his pipe to the next wood. Then he calmly went on playing his pipe.

Meanwhile I marched along rapidly, for it was beginning to grow dark. The birds, which had gone on singing as long as the sun's last rays were shining into the wood, suddenly became quiet, and I began to be almost afraid, amid the endless rustling of the trees. Then at last I heard dogs barking in the distance. I strode quickly on, the wood grew lighter and lighter, and soon I saw through the last few trees a lovely green, and a lot of children were noisily playing around a tall linden in the middle of it. Further off stood an inn in front of which some peasants were sitting round a table and playing cards and smoking. Outside the door on the other side young lads and girls were sitting, the girls with their arms wrapped in their aprons, and chattering away in the cool of the evening.

I wasted no time in thought, but took up my fiddle and played a cheerful country dance as I came out from the wood. The girls were surprised and the old people laughed until their laughter rang through the wood. When I went to the linden and leant back against it, still playing my fiddle, a secret murmuring and whispering ran through the young people. Eventually the lads put their pipes away, each took his girlfriend and, before I knew what was happening, the young peasants were wheeling expertly round me, the dogs were barking, smocks were flying, and the children were standing round me in a ring, looking curiously into my face and at my fingers moving so nimbly.

When the first waltz was over, I knew as never before what effect a good piece of music can have on a person's whole body. The peasant lads, who previously had been lounging on the benches with their legs stretched out stiffly in front of them and with their pipes in their mouths, were now all at once transformed. They had let their coloured handkerchiefs hang down from their buttonholes and they capered around the girls so nimbly that it was a delight to watch. One of them, who thought he really was someone, fumbled for a long time in his waistcoat, so that the others could see it, and at last brought out a small silver piece which he wanted to press into my hand. That annoyed me, even though at that time I had no money in my pocket. I told him to keep his pennies and said that I was playing out of pure joy to be among people once more. But soon a pretty girl came up to me with a large glass of wine. 'Musicians like a drink,' she said, with a friendly smile. And her pearly teeth gleamed with such charm between her red lips that I would have loved to give her a kiss. She put the wine to her lips, flashing her eyes at me over the glass as she did so, and then held the glass out to me. I drained the glass to the dregs and then struck up once more, at which they all whirled round me happily.

Meanwhile the old folk had stopped playing cards. Then the young ones got tired and started to scatter, until finally it was completely quiet and deserted in front of the inn. Even the girl who had given me the wine went back towards the village, but she walked very slowly and looked round from time to time as though she had forgotten something. Finally she stopped and started searching on the ground, but I could see that when she bent down she was looking back at me from under her arm. I had learned some manners while I was at the palace, so I raced up to her and asked, 'Have you lost something, mademoiselle?'

'Oh no,' she said, blushing all over, 'it was only a rose. Would you like it?' I thanked her and put the rose in my buttonhole. She looked at me in a very friendly way and said,

'You play very well.'

'Yes,' I agreed. 'It is a gift from God.'

'There are very few musicians around here,' she went on, and then hesitated with her eyes cast down. 'You could earn yourself a lot of money here – my father plays the fiddle a little too and he likes to hear tell of foreign parts – and my father is very rich.' Then she gave a laugh and said, 'If only you wouldn't make such strange faces and wag your head about when you're playing!'

'My dear young lady,' I replied, 'please don't talk down to me. As for the movement of the head, that cannot be helped, because it's something all we virtuosi do.'

'Yes, of course,' she said. She was about to say something else when a dreadful racket came from the inn, the door burst open with a great crash, a thin fellow came flying out like a bullet from a gun, and the door was slammed shut again after him.

At the first sound the girl had gone bounding off like a deer and disappeared into the darkness. The man quickly gathered himself up from the ground and let loose an amazingly rapid volley of insults at the inn. 'What?' he shouted. 'I'm drunk, am I? I haven't paid what's chalked up on the filthy slate, haven't I? Rub it all out, rub it all out! Didn't I shave you over the spoon[2] yesterday, and cut your nose? And didn't you bite the rotten spoon in half? Shaving pays off one mark on the slate, the spoon another, sticking-plaster for your nose another! How many wretched marks do I still have to pay for? All right then. I'll leave the whole village, the whole world unshaven! As far as I'm concerned you can all run around with beards, and the good God on the Day of Judgement won't know whether you're Christians or Jews! Yes, hang ourselves in your own beards, you shaggy bears!' At this point he suddenly burst into tears and continued in a pitiable falsetto, 'Do I have to drink water like a wretched fish? Do you call this loving your neighbour? Am I not a man and a brother and a trained surgeon? Oh, you make me so annoyed! And my heart is naturally full of compassion and loving-kindness!' Having said this he began to move away, step by step, since there was no sound from the inn. When he saw me he came rushing towards me with arms outspread. I really think the silly ass wanted to embrace me. I jumped to one side and he stumbled past and on and on, and I heard him talking to himself, sometimes gruffly sometimes gently, in the darkness.

But my thoughts were in a whirl. The girl who had just given me the rose was young, beautiful and rich. I could make my fortune there in no time. And I would have lamb and pork and turkey and a fat goose stuffed with apples. Yes, I could even see the major-domo coming up to me and saying, 'Get outside all that, toll-keeper, get outside all that! Happy the wooing that's not long in doing! The lucky man gets the bride! Stay at home and feather your nest!' Philosophising in this way, I sat down on a stone in the now-deserted green. I did not dare to knock on the door of the inn, since I had no money. The moon was shining brightly, the rustling of the wooded hills came through the stillness of the night, and from time to time a dog barked in the village, which lay further on in the valley, buried under trees and moonlight. I scanned the firmament and saw lonely clouds drifting through the moonlight and from time to time a star falling in the distance. 'The moon is shining also,' I thought, 'above my father's mill and on the lordly white palace. Everything there too has long been calm and still, my beautiful lady is asleep, and the fountains and the trees in the gardens are still rustling as they always used to, and it's all the same whether I am there, or abroad, or dead.' Then suddenly the world seemed to me so terribly wide and vast, and I seemed so utterly alone in it, that I could have wept my heart out.

While I was sitting there I heard the sound of horses' hooves in the distance. I held my breath to listen. It came nearer and nearer, until I could hear the snorting of the horses. Then two riders came up beneath the trees, stopped at the edge of the wood, and spoke quietly but excitedly to each other, as I could tell from their shadows which were suddenly projected across the moonlit green and which gestured now this way now that with their long dark arms. How often, when my now-departed mother told me stories of wild woods and savage robbers, had I secretly wished to have such an adventure myself. Now I was being paid back for my silly, wicked thoughts! I reached stealthily up the linden under which I was sitting until I touched the lowest branch and could swing myself up by it. But half my body was still dangling from the branch, and I was just trying to pull my legs up after me, when one of the horsemen came trotting up behind me. There in the dark foliage I shut my eyes tight and kept quite still. 'Who's there?' he suddenly called out, very close to me now.

'No one!' I yelled, terrified because he had already caught on to me. Nevertheless, I had to laugh to myself to think how cut up the fellows would be when they turned out my empty pockets.

'Oho!' said the robber. 'Then to whom do these two legs belong which I can see hanging down?' There was nothing more to be done.

'They are only the two legs of a poor musician who has lost his way,' I answered, and let myself quickly down to the ground, for I felt silly hanging down from the branch like a broken pitchfork.

The horse shied when I dropped so suddenly from the tree. Its rider patted its neck and said with a laugh, 'Well, we've lost our way too, and that makes us friends. I thought you might possibly help us find the road to B–. You won't lose anything by it.' No matter how much I protested that I did not know where B– was, and that I would much prefer to ask in the inn or take them down to the village, the fellow would not listen to reason. He calmly took a pistol from his belt. It shone beautifully in the moonlight. 'My dear chap,' he said, polishing the barrel of the gun and then holding it up to his eyes for inspection, 'please be so good as to take us to B– yourself.'

Now I was between the devil and the deep blue sea. If I found the way, I should certainly meet up with the gang of robbers and get a beating since I had no money with me. If I failed to find the way, I would get a beating for that. So I did not hesitate long. I took the first good road that went past the inn and away from the village. The rider galloped back to his companion and both of them followed me slowly at a distance. So in this truly stupid way we went on through the moonlight, trusting to luck. The road went deeper into the wood and along a mountainside. From time to time, over the crests of the dark swaying pines I could see down into deep silent valleys, occasionally there was the song of a nightingale, and dogs were barking in the villages in the distance. Far down there was the constant rippling of a river, which glittered now and then in the moonlight. All the time there was the monotonous trampling of the horses and the hum and buzz of the riders behind me, chattering to each other incessantly in a foreign tongue, and the bright moonlight and the shadows of the tree trunks that moved across both riders in turn, making them seem now black, now light, now small and now gigantic. I was utterly confused, as though in a dream from which there was no waking. I went on walking briskly ahead. 'We must,' I thought, 'eventually emerge from the wood and the night.'

At long last reddish streaks of light flew here and there over the sky, very faintly, as when one breathes on a mirror, and a lark was already singing high above the quiet valley. All at once these signs of morning made me more light-hearted, and I lost my fear. But the two riders stretched themselves, and looked round about them, and seemed to realise for the first time that we could hardly be on the right road. They began to gabble to each other again, and I could tell that they were talking about me. In fact it looked as though one of them was beginning to be afraid of me, as though I might be a footpad in disguise who was leading them astray in the wood. That idea amused me, for the lighter it became all about, the more courage I had, especially when we came to a nice glade in the wood. So I looked all around quite fiercely, and whistled once or twice through my fingers, as rogues do when they want to signal to each other.

'Halt!' shouted one of the riders. I gave a start. I turned and saw that they had both dismounted and tied their horses to a tree. One of them rushed towards me, looked me in the face, and then started to laugh fit to burst. I must admit that I was peeved by his quite unreasonable laughter. But he said, 'Well I never! It's the gardener, or I should say the palace toll-keeper!'

I looked at him with my eyes wide open, but I could not remember him. However, I would have been hard-pushed to take account of all the young gentlemen who went in and out of the palace. But he went on, amid continual bursts of laughter, 'That's marvellous! I can see you're taking a holiday, and we need a servant, so if you stay with us you can be on holiday all the time.' I was quite dumbfounded, and at last I said that I had been making my way to Italy. 'To Italy?' he

37

replied. 'That's just where we want to go!'

'Well, if that's so – !' I exclaimed. And in my joy I took out my fiddle and struck up, so that all the birds were roused. But one gentleman seized the other and waltzed round on the grass with him as though he had gone mad.

Then suddenly they both stood still. 'Thank God!' cried one of them. 'I can see already the spire of the church at B–. We'll soon be there now.' He took out his watch, made it strike, shook his head, and make it strike again. 'No,' he said, 'we can't have that. We'd get there too soon, which might have unfortunate results.'

And so they brought out cakes, roast meat and bottles of wine, spread a fine coloured cloth over the grass, stretched themselves out there, and feasted very contentedly. They shared everything very generously with me too, which suited me very well since I had not had a proper meal for days. 'And for your information…' one of them said to me, '…but you still don't know us, do you?' I shook my head. 'Well then, for your information, I am the painter Leonhard, and this is another painter, called Guido.'

I now examined the two painters more closely in the dawn light. One, Leonhard, was tall, slender, and dark-skinned, with lively sparkling eyes. The other was much younger, smaller, and more refined, and dressed in the old German fashion, as the major-domo used to call it, with a white collar and an open neck. His dark brown curls hung down so far that he frequently had to shake them away from his handsome face. When this latter had finished his breakfast, he seized my fiddle, which I had laid down beside me on the ground, sat himself down on a branch of a felled tree, and started to strum on it. Then to that accompaniment he sang as finely as a woodland bird. It pierced my heart:

When the first light starts to steal
Through the calm and misty vale,
Hills and woods start murmuring,
And the tiniest birds take wing!

All the people then and there
Fling their hats into the air.
Let our happy thoughts take wing!
Fling our hats away and sing!

As he sang and played, the red glow of the dawn played charmingly across his rather pale face and his dark, amorous eyes. But I was so tired that, as he sang, all the words and notes became more and more confused in my mind, until at last I fell asleep.

When I came to myself again, I heard the two painters still talking beside me, and the birds singing above me, as in a dream. The morning sun was shining into my closed eyes, so that it seemed both dark and light, as when the sun is shining through red silk curtains. '*Come è bello!*'[3] I heard someone close by me exclaim. I opened my eyes and saw the young painter who was bending over me in the flashing dawn light. Almost all I could see was a pair of large dark eyes through the dangling curls.

I sprang up, for it was broad daylight already. Leonhard looked rather peeved. He had two angry lines across his brow and was urging a quick departure. But the other painter shook the curls away from his face and went on humming a little tune to himself as he bridled his horse, until Leonhard finally burst out laughing, picked up a bottle that was still standing on the grass and poured what was left of the wine into the glasses. 'To a safe arrival!' he cried. They clinked their glasses, which made a very pleasant sound. Then Leonhard flung the empty bottle high into the red morning sky, so that it sparkled in the air.

Eventually they mounted their horses, and once again I marched briskly beside them. Immediately in front of us lay an immeasurable valley, into which we made our way. Everywhere there was a murmuring, a twinkling, and the sound of joyful birdsong! I felt so refreshed and cheerful that I felt I could have flown like a bird down from the mountain into the splendid landscape below.

CHAPTER FOUR

Goodbye to mill and palace and major-domo! Now the wind was whistling round my ears. To left and right villages, towns and vineyards were flashing past so rapidly that I felt quite dizzy. Behind me were the two painters in the coach, in front of me four horses with a magnificent coachman, and here was I up on the box bouncing up and down, often a yard into the air.

And this is how it all came about. When we arrived at B– a tall lean surly man in a thick green woollen coat came over to us, bowed many times to the painters and took us into the village. Under the tall lindens in front of the post-house a fine carriage stood waiting with four horses already hitched. On our way there Leonhard had observed that I had grown out of my clothes. And so now he took some others out of his portmanteau, and I had to put on a waistcoat which was quite new and a frock-coat. They suited me very well, except that they were too long and bulky for me and hung down loosely all round. I also had a new hat which gleamed in the sun as if it had been smeared with fresh butter. Then the strange surly man took the painters' horses by their bridles and led them off, the painters sprang into the coach, I sprang onto the box and we swept away, just as the postmaster, still wearing his nightcap, peeped out of the window. The coachman sounded his horn loudly, and we were on our way to Italy.

I really had a marvellous time up there, like a bird but without having to fly. I did not have to do anything but sit on the box day and night, and sometimes fetch food and drink from the inns, for the painters never stopped anywhere for the night, and during the day they kept the curtains drawn tightly across the windows of the coach as though the sunlight would have killed them. Only occasionally Guido would put his handsome head out of the window and hold a friendly conversation with me, and then laugh at Leonhard who could not bear this and got quite annoyed at our long conversations. Once or twice I nearly got into trouble with my masters. Once when I began to play my fiddle out on the box on a beautiful starry night, and then again because of my tendency to fall asleep. This was quite a surprising thing! I really wanted to see Italy, and every quarter of an hour or so I opened my eyes wide. But I had hardly begun to look around when the sixteen horses' hooves in front of me became confused and entangled like netting, this way and that and crosswise, so that my eyes began to water, and eventually I was overcome by such a terrible and inexorable sleep that there was no fighting against it. By day, by night, in the rain and in the sunshine, whether we were in the Tyrol or in Italy, I would droop to the right or to the left, or backwards over the box. In fact I often let my head sink down so far towards the ground that my hat flew off yet again, and Guido cried out from the coach below me.

I had carried on in this way, I hardly know how, through half the land of the Latins, which is known as Lombardy, when one fine evening we stopped at a country inn. Fresh horses had been ordered from the nearby village, but they would only be ready in a few hours, so the painters got out of the coach and asked to be shown to a private room where they might rest a little and write some letters. I was pleased at this, and I made my way straight into the bar, hoping to eat and drink with my accustomed ease and comfort once again. Everything seemed to be quite slovenly there. The serving-maids were going around with their hair uncombed and with their neckerchiefs hanging loose on their yellow skin. The menservants in blue smocks were sitting at a round table having their evening meal, and now and again they stared at me out of the corners of their eyes. They all had short thick pigtails, and looked like distinguished young gentlemen. 'Well,' I thought to myself, as I ate away busily, 'here you are at last in the land from which those strange people used to come and bring our village priest mousetraps, barometers and paintings. What things there are to see, if we can only get away from our own fireside!'

As I was eating and meditating thus, a little man who had been sitting over a glass of wine in a dark corner of the room suddenly darted up to me like a spider. He was short and hunchbacked and had a large, horrible head with a long aquiline nose and sparse red whiskers, and his powdered hair stood on end all round, as though a storm-wind had blown through it. He wore an old-fashioned, faded frock-coat, short plush knee-breeches, and faded silk stockings. He said he had once been to Germany, and said it was amazing how well he understood German. He sat down beside me and asked about this, that, and the other, taking snuff all the while. Was I ze *servitore*? When would we *arrivare*? Were we *goink* to Rome? But I did not know the answers myself, and anyway could not really understand his gibberish. '*Parlez-vous français?*' I asked him at last in sheer desperation. He shook his huge head, and I was glad of that because I knew no French either. But it was no use. He had set his sights on me and he asked more and more questions. The more we spoke, the less we understood each other. Eventually we both became so heated that at times I thought he was going to peck me with his eagle's beak. Then the maidservants, who had been following all this babble, laughed out loud at us both. But I laid my knife and fork down and went outside. In this foreign land I felt that I and my German tongue had both sunk into the sea a thousand fathoms deep, where all sorts of unknown reptiles were writhing and roaring around and staring and snapping at me.

It was a warm summer's night, just right for a gentle stroll. From the vineyards on the distant slopes snatches of song could be heard, there was the occasional flash of lightning in the distance, and the whole landscape was shimmering in the moonlight. Once or twice I did think I could see a tall dark figure slipping past the hazel tree in front of the house and peering through the branches, but then everything was quiet once again. At that moment Guido came out onto the balcony of the inn. He did not notice me, but played very skilfully on a zither which he must have found in the inn, and sang like a nightingale:

> Men's loud joy has gone to rest.
> Earth is whispering as in dreams
> Wonderfully through the trees
> What the heart has hardly guessed:
> All the grief of olden times
> Strikes so gently that it seems
> Summer lightning in my breast.

He may have gone on singing. I do not know, for I was so tired and the night was so mild that I stretched out on the bench in front of the door and fell fast asleep.

Some hours must have gone by when I was awakened by a post-horn. For a long time it was blowing loudly in my dreams before I was fully aware of it. But then I jumped up. Day was already dawning in the mountains and the morning chill was refreshing. Then I remembered that by this time we ought to have been already on the road. 'Aha!' I thought. 'Today it's my turn to wake them up, and the laugh will be on them. And that sleepy-head Guido will rush out when he hears me outside!' So I went into the little garden, close to the window of my

masters' room, drew myself up to my full height and sang out
cheerfully into the dawn:

When the hoopoe sings away
Dawn cannot be far away.
When the morning's gleaming red
Oh, it's nice to stay in bed!

The window was open, but there was no answer. Only the
night wind was still blowing through the vine tendrils which
reached right into the window. 'What's the meaning of this?'
I cried out in my amazement, and ran into the inn and along
the silent passages and up to the room. Then my heart felt
a sudden pang, for when I flung the door open there was
nothing there! Not a frock-coat, not a hat, not a boot! Only the
zither, which Guido had been playing the previous evening,
hung on the wall, and on the table in the middle of the room
lay a nice full purse with a note attached to it. I took the note
nearer to the window, and then I could hardly believe my eyes,
for it had written on it in large letters: *For the toll-keeper*.

But what good was that if I had lost my cheerful masters for
ever? I shoved the purse into the pocket of my jacket. It
dropped with a thud, as though into a deep well, and pulled
my jacket down at the back. Then I ran out, made a great
hullabaloo, and wakened all the servants. They did not know
what I was on about, and they concluded I had gone mad. But
they got quite a shock too, when they saw the empty nest up
above. No one knew anything of my masters, except one maid
who – so far as I could gather from her gesticulations – had
noticed that Guido, when he was singing the evening before
on the balcony, had suddenly given a loud shout, and then
rushed back into the room where the other gentleman was.

Later, when she woke up in the night, she heard the sound of horses' hooves outside. She peeped out of the little window of her room and saw the humpbacked gentleman who had been talking with me so much the day before. But now he was galloping across the fields on a white horse in the moonlight, bouncing out of his saddle a yard into the air. She had made the sign of the cross because he looked like a ghost on a three-legged horse. So now I had no idea what to do.

Meanwhile our coach had been standing for a long time outside the door with its horses hitched, and the coachman was blowing his horn fit to burst in his impatience, for he had to get to the next station on time, since everything had been specially ordered in advance down to the last minute. I ran all over the inn once more and called out to the painters, but there was no answer. People from the inn crowded together outside and gaped at me, the coachman swore, the horses snorted, and at last in sheer confusion I sprang into the coach, the boots slammed the door after me, the coachman cracked his whip, and off I went again into the wide wide world.

CHAPTER FIVE

We travelled on day and night over mountain and valley. I had no time to consider, for when we arrived anywhere the horses were already harnessed, and I could not speak with anyone and my gesticulations did not get me anywhere. Often enough, I had just settled down to my meal in an inn when the coachman blew his horn and I had to drop my knife and fork and jump into the coach again. I had no idea where I was going to in such a great hurry, or why.

Otherwise it was not such a bad way to live. I lay down as though I were on a sofa, first in one corner of the coach and then in the other, and got to know different people and districts, and when we went through towns I leant both arms on the window, looking out and thanking the people who politely took off their hats to me, or greeting like an old friend the girls sitting in the windows, so that they were always amazed and gazed after me for a long while in sheer curiosity.

But eventually I began to be alarmed. I had never counted what money was in the purse, and I had had to pay out a lot to the postmasters and innkeepers everywhere, so before I knew where I was the purse was empty. At first I had the idea of jumping out of the coach and running away as soon as we came to a lonely wood. But then I thought it would be a pity to leave that fine coach all by itself, when we might have gone on together to the ends of the earth.

Just as I was sitting there, without any notion what to do, the coach suddenly swerved off the highway. I shouted out to the coachman and asked him where he was going. But whatever I said, all he would say was, *'Sì, sì, signore!'* And we hurtled on over stocks and stones, so that I was flung from one corner of the coach to the other.

This did not appeal to me at all. The highway ran through beautiful countryside and towards the setting sun, as if into a sea of sparkling light, but the way we were now travelling led to a range of barren mountains, cleft by evil-looking ravines where night had already fallen. The further we went, the wilder and lonelier the land became. When at last the moon came from behind the clouds and shone down brightly on the rocks and trees it was really terrible to see. We had to go slowly through the narrow rocky ravines, and the monotonous everlasting rattle of the coach resounded against the rocky slopes and far into the night, as though we were travelling into a great burial vault. Only from invisible waterfalls further into the wood there came a continual murmur, and owls were all the time calling out in the distance. Then I realised for the first time that the coachman had no uniform and was not really a coachman. He started to look round uneasily and drive faster. When I leaned right out of the window I saw a horseman ride suddenly out of the bushes, cross our path very close to our horses, and disappear in the wood on the other side. I was quite confused for, as far as I could see by the bright light of the moon, it was the same hunchbacked man on the white horse who had pecked at me in the inn with his eagle's beak. The coachman shook his head and laughed out loud at this reckless riding. He turned round quickly to me and talked a lot in great excitement, although I understood none of it, and then drove on even faster.

But then I was overjoyed to see a light shining in the distance. There were more and more lights, which became bigger and bigger and brighter and brighter, and eventually we came to some smoke-blackened huts clinging like swallows' nests to the rocks. The doors stood open, for the night was mild, and I could see inside the brightly lit rooms where all

48

sort of ragged folk were squatting round their hearths like dark shadows. But we rattled on through the silent night, past the hovels and onto a stony track that went up a high mountain. One moment tall trees and overhanging bushes covered the sunken track, and the next the whole of the firmament was visible, with the broad calm expanse of mountains, woods and valleys below. On the mountain peak, a huge ancient castle with many towers stood in the bright moonlight. 'Now God help me!' I cried out, becoming quite excited and wondering where they would bring me to in the end. It was a good half-hour before we got to the castle on the mountain. We went in through a large round tower, all ruined at the top. The coachman cracked his whip three times, which re-echoed throughout the ancient castle, and brought a sudden swarm of jackdaws out of every nook and cranny, criss-crossing the air with a great noise. Then the coach rolled into the long dark passage which led from the gate. The horses' shoes struck sparks from the stone pavement, a large dog barked, and the coach thundered along the vaulted passageway. The jackdaws were still crying out. And so with a hideous racket we came out into the narrow, paved courtyard.

'This is a strange post-house,' I thought, as the coach came to a stop. Then the door of the coach was opened from outside and a tall old man with a small lantern looked at me in a surly way from under his bushy eyebrows. He took me by the arm and helped me out of the coach, as though I were a nobleman. Outside the door stood an old, very ugly woman in a black dress and jacket, with a white apron and cap from which a long ribbon hung down to her nose. A large bunch of keys was hanging by her side and she held an old-fashioned candelabrum with two wax candles burning in it. The moment she saw me she made several very low curtseys, and then she kept on talking to me and asking me questions. I understood nothing of what she said, but kept on bowing and scraping to her, and feeling very uneasy, to tell the truth.

The old man, meanwhile, had been shining his lantern all round the coach, and grumbling and shaking his head because he could find no luggage. Then the coachman, without demanding a tip from me, drove the coach into an old coach-house which stood ready open at one side of the courtyard. The old woman indicated with many polite signs that I should follow her. By the light of her wax candles she led me through a long narrow passage and then up a short flight of stone steps. As we went by the kitchen a couple of young maidservants poked their heads curiously through the half-open door to stare at me, and gave each other secret nods and winks, as though they had never seen such a character before in their lives. When the old woman finally opened a door upstairs, I was quite dumbfounded. It was a huge splendid manorial chamber with a ceiling decorated in gold and walls hung with magnificent tapestries depicting all sorts of figures and large flowers. In the middle of the room stood a table laid with roast meat, cake, salad, fruit, wine and sweetmeats. It was enough to make the heart leap for joy. Between the two windows hung an enormous mirror that went from floor to ceiling.

I must admit that all this pleased me. I stretched myself once or twice and then strode back and forth a few times in a lordly manner. And then I could not resist taking a glance at myself in such a large mirror. The new clothes from Leonhard certainly suited me very well, and my time in Italy had given me a fiery look in the eyes, but otherwise I was the same greenhorn I had been at home, except that there was now a touch of down on my upper lip.

The old woman kept on mumbling away with her toothless

mouth. She looked as though she were chewing the tip of her nose which hung down to her lips. Then she signed to me to sit down, stroked my chin with her thin fingers and called me *poverino!*[4] At the same time she looked at me so archly with her red eyes that one corner of her mouth stretched halfway up her cheek. At last she made a low curtsey and went out of the room.

I sat down at the table, and a pretty young maidservant came to wait on me. I tried to flirt with her in all sorts of ways, but she did not understand me. She gave me rather odd looks out of the corner of her eyes as I relished the delicious food. When I had satisfied my hunger and had risen from the table, she took a lamp and led me into another room. In it was a sofa, a small mirror, and a splendid bed with green silk curtains. In sign language I asked her if I was to lie down. She nodded in agreement, but it was not possible for me to do so, since she remained there as though rooted to the spot. Finally I brought a large glass of wine from the dining room and cried out to her, *'Felicissima notte!'*[5] (This was as far as I had got in my Italian.) But when I drained the glass in one gulp she burst into a fit of suppressed giggles, turned bright red, and went into the dining-room, closing the door behind her. 'What is so funny?' I asked myself. 'I think all the people in Italy must be mad.'

The only thing that worried me now was that the coachman might suddenly start blowing his horn again. I went to the window to listen, but all was quiet outside. 'Well, let him blow,' I thought, as I undressed and climbed into the splendid bed. This was certainly a land flowing with milk and honey! Outside my window the old linden was rustling in the court-yard and from time to time the odd jackdaw flew up from the roof. At last I fell happily asleep.

CHAPTER SIX

When I awoke once more the first light of morning was shining on the green curtains. And I simply could not remember where I was. It was as though I were still travelling in the coach, dreaming of a castle in the moonlight and an old witch and her pale daughter.

At last I jumped out of bed and got dressed, looking all around the room as I did so. It was then that I noticed a small door behind a curtain, which I had failed to see the day before. It was just closed to, so I opened it and saw into a neat little room which looked very cosy in the half-light of dawn. There were some women's clothes thrown haphazardly over a chair, and in a small bed nearby lay the maidservant who had waited on me the previous evening. She was still fast asleep, with her head on her bare white arm, over which hung her black curly hair. 'If she only knew the door was open!' I thought, and I went back into my bedroom, closing the door and bolting it behind me, lest she should feel frightened and disconcerted when she awoke.

There was no sound outside but the morning song of an early woodland bird perched on a bush growing out of the wall under my window. 'No,' I said, 'I won't let you put me to shame, singing so alone and diligently and praising God so early in the morning!' I snatched up my fiddle, which I had left on the table the night before, and went outside. There was a deathly hush throughout the castle, and it took me a long while to find my way outside through the dark corridors.

Once outside, I came upon a large garden, which went halfway down the mountainside in a series of broad terraces. But the garden was in a sad state. The paths were all overgrown with high grass, and the topiary figures of the box trees had not been trimmed. Like ghosts they stretched their long noses and pointed hoods into the air, which in the half-light was really frightening. There was even some washing hanging over broken statues by a dried-up fountain, cabbages had been planted here and there in the middle of the garden, and there were a few common-or-garden flowers. Everything was higgledy-piggledy and overgrown with tall weeds, with brightly coloured lizards slithering among them. However, through the old tall trees lay a broad open prospect, one mountain peak after another, as far as the eye could see.

When I had been strolling round in the half-light through this wilderness for some time, I saw on the terrace below me a tall, slender, pale youth in a long brown hooded gown who was striding up and down with his arms folded. He appeared not to have seen me, for he sat himself down on a stone bench, took a book out of his pocket and read from it out loud, as though he were preaching, looking up to heaven from time to time, and then laid his head to rest on his right hand in a melancholy way. I looked at him a long while. Then, curious to know why he was making such strange faces, I walked over to him quickly. He had just given vent to a deep sigh, and when I arrived he jumped up in alarm. He was very embarrassed, and so was I, neither of us knew what to say, and we kept on bowing to each other, until finally he took to his heels and ran off into the bushes. Meanwhile the sun had risen above the wood, and so I jumped up on the bench and struck up on my fiddle in sheer joy, making it resound far down below in the silent valleys. The old woman with the bunch of keys, who had been anxiously searching for me in the castle to serve me my breakfast, now appeared on the terrace above me and was amazed that I could play the fiddle so well. The surly old man from the castle was there too, and was also amazed. Finally the maids came, and then they all stood still above me, full of wonder. And I fingered my fiddle and waved my fiddle-bow about more and more artistically and rapidly, and played cadenzas and variations, until at last I was tired out.

But there was something very strange about the castle! No one thought of travelling on from it. Also, it was not just an inn, but belonged, as I gathered from the maid, to a rich count. When, on occasion, I asked the old woman the name of the count and where he lived, she merely smirked, as she had on my first evening, and blinked and winked at me in such a sly manner that I thought she was losing her wits. If on a hot day I drank a whole bottle of wine, then the maids were sure to giggle when they brought another, and once when I was longing for a pipeful of tobacco, and I made it clear by signs what I wanted, they all burst out into senseless laughter. The most strange thing, however, was the sound of music by night, and always on the darkest nights, which could often be heard below my window. Someone was striking up softly from time to time on a guitar. On one occasion it seemed to me that I heard from below, 'Pst, pst!' I rushed out of bed and put my head out of the window. 'Hello, hello! Who's out there?' I shouted down. But there was no answer and I heard something running away very quickly through the bushes. The big dog in the courtyard added his barking to the noise once or twice, and then suddenly everything was quiet once more, and I never heard the music again after that.

Apart from that, I led such a life that no one could have wished for better. That major-domo! He certainly knew what he was talking about when he used to say that in Italy the raisins just dropped into one's mouth. I lived in the lonely castle like an enchanted prince. Wherever I went people showed me great respect, although they all knew by now that I had not a farthing to my name. I had only to say, 'Table, set yourself!' and I found splendid food, rice, wine, melons and Parmesan cheese laid out on it. I really enjoyed my meals, slept in the splendid four-poster, strolled in the garden, played my music, and sometimes even helped with the gardening. Often I would lie for hours in the garden in the tall grass, and the slender youth (he was a student and a relative of the old people, who was here on holiday) described wide circles round me in his long gown, murmuring all the while, like a magician, from his book, so that I always fell asleep. So one day went by after another until, what with the good food and drink, I became rather melancholy. My limbs felt quite out of joint from this everlasting idleness, and I felt as if I would fall apart from sheer laziness.

One sultry afternoon I was sitting at the top of a tall tree that grew on the slope of the mountain, and rocking myself gently in the branches over the deep silent valley. Except for the bees humming round me in the foliage, all was as silent as the grave, there was no one to be seen on the hills, and far below the cattle were lying on the deep grass in the meadows. But then there came the sound of a distant post-horn over the wooded heights, at first so low it was hardly perceptible, and then higher and more distinct. At that, an old song came into my mind, which I had learned at home from a travelling worker at my father's mill, and I sang out:

> *Who goes among foreign people*
> *Must go with a love of his own.*
> *The others are glad to ignore him,*
> *The stranger standing alone.*

You know nothing, you gloomy treetops,
Of the happy times of yore.
Oh, my home beyond the mountains
Is so very far from here!

I love to look up at the starlight,
Which shone when I went to her,
And I love the nightingale's singing,
Which I heard at my loved one's door.

I am happiest in the morning!
I climb at an early hour
To the top of the highest mountain
And greet Germany from afar.

The post-horn in the distance seemed to be accompanying my song. While I was singing, its sound came closer and closer between the mountains, until I heard it resounding in the courtyard of the castle. I clambered quickly down from my tree. Then the old woman came towards me from the castle with an opened packet in her hand. 'There's something come with this for you too,' she said and handed me a dainty little letter from the packet. It had no address on it. I opened it quickly. Then my face went as red as a beetroot, and my heart beat so loudly that the old woman noticed it, for the letter was from my beautiful lady! I had seen her handwriting on many notes in the steward's office. The letter was very short:

Everything is all right again now. All obstacles have been removed. I am secretly seizing this opportunity to be the first to give you the good news. Please hurry back. It is so tedious here, and I have hardly been able to go on living since you left.

– Aurelie.

In rapture and trepidation and ineffable joy my eyes filled with tears. I felt ashamed in front of the old woman, who was once again smirking at me horribly, so I shot like an arrow to the loneliest corner of the garden. Then I threw myself down on the grass under the hazel bushes and read the letter again, said every word by heart, and then read it again and yet again, and the sunbeams shone through the leaves and danced over the words, so that the individual letters twisted in and out of each other like gold and bright green and red flowers. 'Perhaps she isn't really married after all?' I wondered. 'Perhaps the foreign officer was her brother, or perhaps he is dead now, or perhaps I'm mad, or…' 'But it's all the same!' I cried out at last, and jumped up. 'One thing is clear. She loves me, she loves me!'

By the time I crawled out from under the bushes, the sun was starting to set. The heavens were red, the birds were singing in all the woods, and the valleys were filled with shimmering light, but in my heart everything was a thousand times more beautiful and happy!

I shouted into the castle for them to bring my supper out to the garden. The old woman, the surly old man, the maids – they all had to come out and join me at my table under the tree. I took out my fiddle and played, and ate and drank in between times. Then everyone was happy. The old man smoothed the surly wrinkles on his face and emptied glass upon glass, the old woman went on chattering about the Lord knows what, and the maids began to dance with each other on the lawn. Eventually even the pale student came along out of curiosity, cast a disdainful glance at the spectacle and began to move away. But I lost no time in jumping up, seizing him by his long overcoat, before he knew what was happening, and waltzing madly round with him. He tried hard to dance neatly in the modern fashion, and moved his feet about so industriously and artistically that the sweat ran down his face and his long coat-tails flew round us like the spokes of a wheel. Meanwhile he was looking at me so strangely with his rolling eyes that I began to feel afraid of him, and all at once I let him go.

The old woman was desperate to know what was in the letter and why I had suddenly become so joyful today. But that was too complicated to explain, so I merely pointed to a pair of cranes that happened to be flying over us and said, 'I too will have to go on and on far away.' Then she opened her dry old eyes wide and stared like a basilisk, now at me and now at the old man. Then I noticed that, whenever I turned away, they put their heads together stealthily and talked excitedly, looking at me askance from time to time.

That surprised me. I could not think what they intended to do about me. But I soon stopped worrying. The sun had long since set, and I said goodnight to everyone and went up thoughtfully to my bedroom.

I was so happy and restless that I walked up and down in my room for a long while. Outside the wind was sweeping heavy black clouds over the castle tower, and it was so dark that even the nearest mountain peaks could scarcely be seen. Then I thought I heard voices in the garden below. I extinguished my lamp and went to the window. The voices seemed to be coming nearer, but they were speaking very softly. Suddenly light shone out from a small lantern which one of the figures was carrying under his cloak, and now I recognised the surly steward of the castle and the old housekeeper. The light flashed over the face of the old woman, who looked more hideous than ever, and onto a long knife which she was holding. And I could see that they were both looking up at my window. Then the steward pulled his cloak round himself more closely, and all was once more dark and quiet.

'What were they doing,' I asked myself, 'outside in the garden at this hour?' I shuddered, thinking of all the murderous tales I had heard of witches and robbers who slaughtered people in order to feed on their hearts. While I was lost in these thoughts, I heard footsteps, first coming up the stairs, then along the corridor to my room, and then very softly right up to my door. And I seemed to hear voices whispering secretly to each other. I leapt to the other side of the room and put myself behind a large table. The moment anything moved, I intended to hold the table in front of myself and rush towards the door with all my strength. But in the darkness I knocked over a chair which made a dreadful noise. Everything went quiet outside. From behind the table I went on staring at the door, as though to pierce it with my eyes, which were popping out of my head. When I had managed to stay still for while, so still that the flies could be heard crawling up the wall, I heard someone gently putting a key into the keyhole. I stood ready to let fly with my table, but the key was turned slowly three times and then withdrawn cautiously and I could hear someone shuffling off along the corridor and down the stairs.

Now I could breathe once more. 'Aha!' I thought to myself. 'They have locked me in so as to have easy work of it once I am asleep.' Quickly I examined the door. I was right. It was locked. And so was the other door behind which the pale maidservant slept. That had never happened before, all the time I had been at the castle.

So I had been taken captive in a foreign land! My beautiful lady was no doubt standing at her window now and looking across the quiet gardens towards the highway, hoping that I might come strolling along past the toll-house with my fiddle, the clouds were scurrying across the sky, time was passing –

and I could not get away from here! I felt very sad, and I had no idea what to do. All this time, whenever the leaves rustled outside or a rat gnawed at the floorboards, I seemed to see the old woman creep stealthily in through a secret door hidden by an arras, and lurk about, and steal quietly through the room with her long knife.

As I was sitting on my bed in such misery, I suddenly heard, for the first time in a long while, the night music under my window once more. At the first note of the guitar it was as though a morning sunbeam shone into my soul. I flung the window open and called down softly to indicate that I was awake. 'Pst, pst!' came the answer from below. Without losing any time thinking about it, I gathered up my letter and my fiddle, swung out of the window, and clambered down the old cracked wall, holding onto the bushes which grew out of the cracks. But a few rotten bricks gave way, I started to slide down, I went faster and faster, and at last I landed with a thud and saw stars.

I had scarcely arrived in the garden when someone embraced me so violently that I shouted out loud. But my good friend put his finger to my lips, seized me by the hand, and led me out of the shrubbery into the open. Then I was amazed to see that it was the tall student, with his guitar hanging from his neck by a broad silk ribbon. As quickly as I could, I gave him to understand that I wanted to escape from the garden. He seemed to have known about this all along and brought me by all sorts of hidden, roundabout ways to the lowest gate in the high wall of the garden. But that gate was shut too! However, the student had already thought of this and he took out a large key and opened the gate cautiously.

When we were in the wood and I was about to ask him the way to the nearest town, he suddenly fell down on one knee in front of me, raised one hand high in the air, and began to curse and swear. It was horrible to hear him. I did not know what he wanted, and all I could hear, again and again, was *Iddio* and *cuore* and *amore* and *furore!*[6] But when he went so far as to slither nearer and nearer to me on both knees, I realised to my horror that he must be mad and I ran off in the depths of the forest without looking back.

I could hear the student shouting madly after me. Then another, coarser, voice came from the castle, answering him. I thought that they would start searching for me. I did not know the way, the night was dark, and I could easily fall into their hands again. So I climbed to the top of a tall fir tree to wait for a better opportunity to escape.

From there I could hear one voice after another raised in the castle. Some torches became visible up in the castle and cast their wild red glow over the ancient walls and far into the black night. I commended my soul to God, for the confused uproar became louder and louder and closer and closer. Then the student, with a torch in his hand and his coat-tails flying out behind him in the wind, rushed past beneath my tree. After that they all seemed to turn gradually to the other side of the mountain, their voices sounded further and further off, and once again there was only the wind rustling through the silent wood. I climbed down quickly from my tree and ran breathlessly on into the valley and the night.

CHAPTER SEVEN

I rushed on, day and night, for their cries still rang in my ears as they came down the mountain after me with their torches and long knives. Eventually, when I had covered quite a distance, I gathered that I was only a few miles from Rome. This filled me with joy, for when I was a child at home I had heard many wonderful stories of the splendour of this city. As I lay on the grass outside the mill on Sunday afternoons and everything around was so quiet, I used to think that Rome must be like the clouds moving above me, with wonderful mountains and ravines going down to the blue sea, and golden gates, and tall gleaming towers on which golden-robed angels were singing. Night had fallen long since, and the moon was shining brightly when finally I came out of the wood onto a hilltop and suddenly saw the city in the distance. The sea was glimmering far off, the immeasurable heavens were twinkling and sparkling with their countless stars, and below them lay the Holy City, of which only a long strip of mist was visible, like a sleeping lion on the quiet earth, while the hills stood round like dark giants watching over it.

I came at first to a wide, lonely heath, where everything was as grey and silent as the tomb. Here and there stood an ancient crumbling wall or a withered, strangely contorted bush, birds flew through the night air and my own dark shadow stretched out and out into the loneliness before me. They say that a very ancient city lies buried here and the goddess Venus lies buried in it, and that from time to time the old pagans still rise out of their graves at the dead of night and lead wanderers astray. But I strode on and did not let this bother me. The city now rose up ever more distinct and splendid before me, and the tall palaces and gates and the golden cupolas gleamed in the bright moonlight. It looked as though angels really were standing on the battlements and singing out into the quiet night.

I went past a few small houses and then through a magnificent gate into the renowned city of Rome. The moon shone between the palaces and down into the streets as though it were broad daylight, but the streets were all deserted except for the occasional ragged fellow lying in a marble doorway in the warm night and sleeping like the dead. The fountains were plashing in the silent squares, and the gardens along the street were rustling and filling the air with refreshing scents.

As I sauntered along, so full of satisfaction, moonlight and sweet scents that I did not know where to turn, there came the sound of a guitar from one of the gardens. 'Heavens!' I thought, 'I must have been followed here by the mad student with the long cloak!' Then a lady started to sing sweetly in the garden. I was enchanted, for it was the voice of my beautiful gracious lady, and the song was the same Italian song which she so often used to sing at her open window in the palace. Then all at once the memory of that old happy time overwhelmed me. I felt like weeping as I recalled the silent gardens of the palace in the early morning, and how I used to hide so joyfully behind the bush until that stupid fly flew up my nose. I could not stop myself. I climbed over the gilded decorations on the iron gate and down into the garden from which the singing had come. Then I noticed that a slim white form was standing behind a poplar and looking at me in amazement as I climbed over the gate. Then suddenly it fled through the dark garden and into the house, so swiftly that the movement of the feet was scarcely perceptible in the moonlight. 'That was her!' I shouted out loud, and my heart beat for joy. I had recognised her immediately by her quick little feet. Unfortunately I had also sprained my right foot in jumping off the gate, and so I had to swing my leg about a bit before I could follow her to the house. Meanwhile the doors and windows had all been shut. I knocked softly, listened, and then knocked again. I thought I could hear a low whispering and giggling inside, and once I even imagined I saw two bright eyes sparkle out into the moonlight from behind the shutters. Then everything was quiet once more.

'She cannot know who it is,' I thought. So I took up my fiddle, which I always had with me, strolled up and down on the path in front of the house and played and sang the song of the beautiful lady. In fact, I was glad to play all the songs which I used to play on summer nights in the palace gardens, or on the bench in front of the toll-house, until my singing rang through the windows of the palace. But all this was useless now. Throughout the house no one stirred. So, at last, I sadly laid my fiddle by and stretched myself out on the doorstep, for I was tired out by my long walk. The night was warm, the flower-beds were giving off a sweet scent and a fountain down in the garden was splashing away. I dreamed of sky-blue flowers, of beautiful, dark green, lonely valleys where springs murmured and streams rippled and brightly coloured birds were singing, until at last I fell asleep.

When I awoke I felt the morning air trickling through my whole body. The birds were already awake and chirping in the trees as though they were making fun of me. I jumped up and looked round me on all sides. The fountain was still playing, but in the house there was no sound. I peeped through the green shutters into one of the rooms. In it there was a sofa, a large round table covered with a linen cloth, and chairs standing neatly against the walls, undisturbed. All the shutters had been closed on the windows from the outside, as though the house had not been lived in for many years. Then I felt a sudden horror of the deserted house and garden and of the white figure I had seen the night before. I ran without looking back through the silent pergolas and along the silent paths, and climbed again rapidly up onto the garden gate. Then I sat there thunderstruck, looking down from the gate onto the splendid city below. The morning sun was flashing and sparkling far over the roofs and through the long, silent streets. I gave a great shout of joy and jumped down into the street.

But where was I to turn in this huge, strange city? The confusion of the previous night and the beautiful lady's Italian song kept going through my head. Eventually I sat down on the stone rim of the fountain in the middle of the deserted square, rinsed my eyes in the clear water and sang:

Were I a little bird
I know what I would sing.
And if I had but wings
I know where I would wing.

'Hello, young fellow, you're just like a lark, singing at the crack of dawn!' said a young man, who had meanwhile come up to the fountain. For me, when I so unexpectedly heard German spoken, it was as though I caught the sound of the church-bells in my village suddenly ringing out on a quiet Sunday morning. 'God bless you, my fellow countryman!' I exclaimed delightedly, leaping down from the fountain. The young man smiled and looked me up and down. 'Well, what are you doing here in Rome?' he asked finally. I did not know quite what to say, for I did not want to tell him I was in pursuit of my beautiful lady. 'I'm just wandering about, hoping to see something of the world.' 'Is that so?' replied the young man, laughing out loud. 'Then we're in the same line of work. That's just what I'm doing. I want to see the world and then paint it.' 'So you're a painter?' I exclaimed happily, with Leonhard and Guido in mind. But he would not let me speak. 'I think,' he said, 'that you should come and have breakfast at my place. Then I shall make a really good painting of you.' I was pleased at this, and so I went with the painter through the empty streets. Only here and there a few shop windows were being opened, and now and again a pair of white arms was to be seen, or a sleepy face peered out into the fresh morning air.

He led me through a lot of twisting, narrow, dark alleys, until at last we slipped into an old smoke-blackened house. Then we climbed one dark staircase after another, as if we were ascending into heaven. At last we reached the attic, and we stood in front of the door while the painter hastily searched in all his pockets for the key. But when he went out early that morning he had forgotten to lock the door and his key was in the room. As he had told me on our way there, he had gone out before daybreak to see the sunrise. So he merely shook his head and kicked the door open.

It was a very long, broad room, and would have been big enough to dance in, had the entire floor not been covered with all kinds of things. There were boots, papers, clothes, over-turned paint-pots, all mixed up. In the middle of the room stood some large structures, like those used for picking pears, and large pictures were leaning against the walls all round. On the long wooden table there was a dish with bread and butter on it and a splash of paint, and by the dish a bottle of wine.

'Eat and drink first, my fellow-countryman!' cried the painter to me. I did feel like having a few slices of bread and butter immediately, but there was no knife there. We had to grope around among the papers on the table for a long while before we found one under a large parcel. Then the painter flung the window open, so that the fresh morning air swirled through the whole room. There was a marvellous outlook over the city and towards the mountains, with the early sun shining on the white villas and vineyards. 'Here's to our cool green Germany beyond those mountains!' cried the painter, drinking from the bottle which he then passed to me. I responded to him politely and in my heart I thought again and again of my beautiful distant home.

Meanwhile the painter had brought one of the wooden structures, on which a large piece of paper was stretched, over to the window. On the paper there was a drawing of an old hut, made with a few black strokes. Inside the hut sat the Holy Virgin with a joyful and yet very sad look on her beautiful face. At her feet in a bed of straw lay the Christ Child, with large, kind, earnest eyes. Outside on the threshold of the hut's open door two shepherd boys were kneeling with their staffs and knapsacks. 'Look,' said the painter, 'I'm going to put your head on one of these shepherd boys. So your face will become known to people and, God willing, they will get some pleasure from it when we have both been dead a long while and are kneeling calmly and happily before our Holy Mother and her Son, just like the shepherd boys here.' He seized an old chair, part of the back of which came off in his hand as he tried to lift it. He put it quickly back together again and shoved it in front of the structure, and I had now to sit on it with my face half turned towards him. For a few minutes I sat quite still. But at last, I do not know why, I could not bear it any longer. I started to itch, now here, now there. Also, right opposite me there was half a broken mirror which I had to look into all the time, and while he was painting me I kept pulling all kinds of faces in it out of sheer boredom. The painter noticed this, laughed out loud, and then gestured with his hand for me to stand up again. My face was already on the shepherd boy, and it was such a likeness that even I was pleased with myself.

In the cool fresh morning air he went on sketching industriously, singing as he did so, and at times looking out into the beautiful countryside. I cut myself another sandwich and walked contentedly round the room with it, looking at the pictures leaning against the walls. Two of them struck me as particularly good ones. 'Did you paint these too?' I asked. 'What an idea!' he answered. 'They are by the famous masters Leonardo da Vinci and Guido Reni. But I'm sure you know nothing about all them!' That last remark annoyed me, and I retorted calmly, 'I know both those masters like the back of my hand.' He goggled. 'How?' he asked quickly. 'Well,' I said, 'didn't I travel with them day and night, on horseback, on foot and by coach, with the wind whistling round my ears? And didn't I lose them both at the inn? And didn't I travel on in their carriage by special mail-coach, with the confounded vehicle flying along on two wheels over the horrible stones, and –' 'Oho, oho!' he interrupted, staring at me as though he thought I was mad. But then he suddenly burst out laughing. 'Now at last I understand,' he said. 'You have travelled with two painters called Guido and Leonhard?' When I agreed that this was so, he leapt to his feet and looked me up and down very carefully. 'I do believe it,' he said. 'And you play the violin too?' I struck my pocket and my fiddle twanged inside it. 'Well,' said the painter, 'a German countess has been here, enquiring in every nook and cranny of Rome after the two painters and the young musician with his fiddle.' 'A young German countess?' I cried out in delight. 'Is the major-domo with her?' 'I know nothing of that,' replied the painter. 'I only saw them a few times at the house of a friend of hers who doesn't even live in the city. Do you know her?' All of a sudden he pulled a canvas cover off a large picture in a corner of the room. To me it was as though someone had opened the shutters in a dark room and let the morning sunlight in. It was the beautiful lady! She was wearing a black velvet dress and standing in a garden, lifting her veil from her face with one hand, and looking out into the glorious countryside with a calm and kindly expression on her face. The longer I gazed the more it looked to me like the palace garden, with the flowers and branches swaying gently in the wind, with down below in the distance my little toll-house and the highway stretching out over the green countryside, and the Danube and the blue mountains in the distance.

'It's her, it's her!' I shouted. I snatched up my hat and ran out of the door and down the many flights of stairs, with the amazed painter crying after me that if I came back that evening we might perhaps be able to find out more.

CHAPTER EIGHT

I ran through the city as fast as I could go, to get to the house where I had heard the beautiful lady singing the evening before. On the streets everything had livened up – ladies and gentlemen were walking in the sunshine and bowing and greeting each other, splendid coaches were rattling along, and in the church towers the bells were ringing out for Mass, their peals resounding in the clear air above all the hurly-burly. I ran on, drunk with happiness at all the noise around me. In my joy I ran straight on, until eventually I did not know where I was any longer. Everything seemed to have been under a spell, as though the quiet square with the fountain, and the garden, and the house had been only a dream, and all had disappeared from the world in the bright light of day.

I could not ask the way, for I did not know the name of the square. Eventually it became very sultry too, the sun's rays struck against the pavement like scorching arrows, people crept into their homes, every shutter was closed, and all at once there was no sign of life in the street. In desperation I threw myself down in front of a fine large house with a pillared balcony that cast a wide shadow. I gazed now at the silent city, whose sudden emptiness in the bright midday seemed very weird, and then at the deep blue, almost cloudless, sky, until finally I fell asleep from sheer weariness. I dreamed I was lying in my village in a lonely green meadow, warm summer rain was sparkling and shining in the sun as it set behind the mountains, and as the raindrops fell onto the grass they kept turning into beautifully coloured flowers, until they covered me completely.

But I was truly astonished when I awoke, for I saw a mass of beautiful fresh flowers literally on me and all round me.

I jumped up, but could see nothing unusual except, in the house above me, a wide-open window full of sweetly scented shrubs and flowers, behind which a parrot was incessantly chattering and shrieking. I gathered up the scattered flowers, tied them together and put the nosegay into my buttonhole. Then I started a discussion with the parrot, for I enjoyed watching him climbing up and down in his gilded cage, making all sorts of grimaces, and walking so clumsily on his pigeon-toes. But I was surprised to hear him scold me and call out to me, *'Furfante!'*[7] He may have been a beast without the use of reason, but it annoyed me all the same. I responded in kind and we both became heated. The more I abused him in German, the more he burbled on at me in Italian.

Just then I heard someone laughing behind me. I turned round quickly. It was the painter I had met in the morning. 'What's this you're doing now?' he asked. 'I've been waiting for you half an hour already. The air is cooler now, so let us go to a garden outside the city where you will find more fellow-countrymen and perhaps discover something further about the German countess.'

I was more than pleased to hear this, and off we set. For a long while I could still hear the parrot abusing me behind my back.

We walked for quite a time outside the town and up narrow stony footpaths between villas and vineyards until we came to an elevated garden where several young men and women were sitting at a round table which had been set up on the grass. As we entered the garden they all gestured to us to make no noise and pointed to the other side of the garden. There, in a large vine-covered arbour, two ladies were sitting opposite each other at a table. One was singing and the other accompanied her on a guitar. Between the two and behind the table stood a kindly man who beat time now and then with a small baton. The evening sun was glittering down through the vine leaves onto the wine bottles and fruit with which the table was covered and over the full round dazzlingly white shoulders of the lady with the guitar. The other lady was enraptured, and she sang in Italian with such exceptional art that the sinews stood out on her neck.

Just as she was singing a long cadenza, with her eyes held up to heaven, and the man by her with his baton raised was waiting for her to pick up the time again, and no one in the garden was daring to breathe, the garden gate was suddenly flung open and a girl with a flushed face followed by a young man with a delicate pale countenance rushed in, quarrelling furiously. The astonished conductor stood there with baton on high like a magician turned to stone, even though the singer had broken off her lengthy trill some time ago and had risen angrily. All the others were hissing furiously at the young man. 'Barbarian!' shouted one of the men sitting at the round table. 'You're rushing right into the middle of an ingenious tableau of the beautiful description by the late lamented E.T.A. Hoffmann, on page 347 of *The Lady's Magazine* for 1816, of Hummel's most beautiful painting which could be seen in the Berlin exhibition in the autumn of 1814!' But this did no good at all. 'What do I care,' the young man answered, 'about your tableaux of tableaux? A personally designed picture for the others, and my girl for me alone – that's my principle!' Then he went on again at the poor young girl, 'You faithless one, you traitor! You fastidious soul, who look in the art of painting only for the gleam of silver, and in the art of poetry only for the golden thread, and have not loved a single person, but only a heap of treasure! Henceforth, instead of an honest fool of a painter, I hope you get an old duke with a whole ruby mine on his nose, a touch of silver on his bald pate, and gilt ends on his few remaining hairs! Now come on, out with that wretched piece of paper that you've just hidden from me! What have you been plotting? Who's the note from, and who's it for?'

But the girl resisted steadfastly, and the more eagerly the others surrounded the furious young fellow and tried to comfort and calm him with their great noise, the more heated and crazed he became with all the racket, particularly since the girl could not hold her tongue and finally burst out of the confused mass of people and quite suddenly and unexpectedly threw herself upon my breast for protection. I at once assumed the appropriate attitude but, since the others paid no attention to us in all the uproar, she suddenly looked up at me and whispered softly and rapidly in my ear, with a completely calm expression on her face, 'You abominable toll-keeper! It's because of you I have to suffer all this. Take this wretched note quickly. You will find our address on it. And when you come through the gate at the appointed hour, keep going on the lonely road that turns to the right!'

In my amazement I could hardly speak, for now that I looked at her properly I suddenly recognised her. She was in fact the cheeky chambermaid from the palace who had brought me the bottle of wine on that beautiful Saturday evening. She had never looked so pretty as she did then, flushed, leaning on me, with her black curls falling over my arm. 'But, my dear mademoiselle,' I asked, 'how do you come –' 'For heaven's sake, keep quiet!' she replied, and sprang away to the other side of the garden, before I realised what was happening.

The others meanwhile had almost completely forgotten the original subject of discussion, but they went on arguing with each other very contentedly, trying to convince the young fellow that he was really drunk, which they thought was not appropriate behaviour for a self-respecting painter. The rotund, energetic man from the arbour – who, as I discovered later, was a great connoisseur and friend to the arts, and out of sheer love of all branches of knowledge was happy to join in anything – had thrown his baton away and was striding about eagerly, with his fat face gleaming with bonhomie, in the very thick of the tumult. He was trying to act as a mediator and smooth everything down, while at the same time he kept on deploring the loss of the long cadenza and the beautiful tableau which he had worked so hard to arrange.

But in my heart all was as bright as the stars, just as it was on that happy Saturday when I sat at the open window with my bottle of wine and played my fiddle far into the night. When it seemed that the noise would never end, I snatched up my fiddle and played impromptu an Italian tune which they dance to in the mountains and which I had learned while I was in the lonely castle in the woods.

And then they all raised their heads. 'Bravo, bravissimo! A marvellous idea!' cried out the happy connoisseur of all the arts, and he started running from one person to another, to arrange a 'rustic *divertimento*', as he called it. He started it off by offering his hand to the lady who had been playing the guitar in the arbour. He then began to dance with exceptional expertise, describing all sorts of figures on the lawn and even quavering with his feet, and cutting tolerable capers from time to time. But he had soon had enough, for he was rather corpulent. His capers became briefer and briefer and more and more awkward, until eventually he retired from the circle, puffing violently and continually wiping the sweat off his face with his snow-white handkerchief. Meanwhile the young fellow, who had by now quite calmed down, fetched some castanets from the inn, and in an instant they were all dancing happily with one another beneath the trees. The setting sun was still casting some red reflections between the dark shadows and across the old walls and the half-sunken, ivy-covered columns in the background, while from the other side far below the vineyards, the city of Rome was visible in the evening glow. They all danced harmoniously in the clear still air, and my heart was tickled to see the slender girls, the chambermaid among them, skipping through the foliage with their arms raised like pagan wood nymphs, and snapping their castanets in the air at every step. I could not contain myself any longer. I leapt into the middle of them and, without pausing in my playing, I too performed some very graceful steps.

I sprang around in the dance for quite a while, and I failed to notice that the others had begun to get tired and were gradually leaving the lawn. Then someone gave a good pull at my coat-tails from behind. It was the chambermaid. 'Stop playing the fool,' she said softly. 'You're leaping about like a billy-goat. Take a proper look at the note and follow along after me very soon. The beautiful young countess is waiting.' And therewith she slipped away in the dusk through the garden gate and was soon lost to sight among the vineyards.

My heart was throbbing, and I felt like running straight after her. Fortunately the waiter, since it was by now quite dark, had lit a large lantern which hung over the garden gate. I went up to it and took out the note. On it was a rough pencil-sketch showing the gate and the road, as the chambermaid had told me, and the words: 'Eleven o'clock at the small door.'

There were still several long hours to go! Nevertheless I felt like setting off immediately, for I could not contain myself. But then the painter who had brought me there came up to me. 'Have you spoken with the girl?' he asked. 'I can't see her about any more. She's the German countess' chambermaid.' 'That's all right,' I said. 'The countess is still in Rome.' 'All the better,' he said. 'Come with us and drink her health!' And, despite my resistance, he pulled me back into the garden.

That was now all empty and dreary. The happy guests were wandering back to the city, each with his loved one on his arm, and they could be heard in the quiet evening as they chattered and laughed on their way past the vineyards. As they went on into the distance, their voices became fainter and fainter, until at last they were lost in the murmuring of the trees and the stream in the valley far below. Now I was left alone with my painter and with Eckbrecht, the other young painter who had previously been quarrelling with everyone. The moon shone brightly into the garden through the tall dark trees, a light was flickering in the wind on the table in front of us and gleaming on all the wine which had been spilt there. I had to sit down with them while my painter chattered to me about my background, my journey and my purpose in life. Eckbrecht, however, had taken the pretty young waitress on his knee, after she had put some bottles on the table for us, and was teaching her to strum on the guitar. Her tiny hands soon learned how to manage the instrument, and then they sang together an Italian song, taking alternate stanzas, which was very delightful in the lovely quiet evening. When the girl was called away, Eckbrecht took the guitar, leaned back on the bench, put his feet up on a chair in front of him and sang many splendid German and Italian songs to himself without bothering any further with us. The stars were shining brightly in the clear sky, all the countryside around was silver in the moonlight, and I thought about the beautiful lady and my distant home, and completely forgot the painter beside me. At times Eckbrecht had to tune his guitar and this made him quite angry. He twisted the instrument and pulled at it so much that he broke a string. He threw the guitar away and jumped up. It was then that he realised for the first time that my painter had laid his arm on the table and laid his head on his arm and fallen fast asleep. He threw about himself a white cloak which had been hanging on a branch of a tree near the table, suddenly hesitated, looked at my painter, and then several times at me very sharply, sat down without further consideration at the table in front of me, cleared his throat, tugged at his cravat, and started on a long speech: 'Dear listener and fellow-countryman,' he said, 'since the bottles are almost empty, and since moralising is indisputably the first duty of a citizen when virtues are running short, I feel it incumbent upon myself, out of patriotism and fellow-feeling, to instil into your mind some moral values. One might think you were a mere lad, although your coat has seen better days. One might perhaps admit that you have just been leaping about like a satyr. Yes, some might even maintain that you are a vagrant, since you are here on the fiddle, so to speak. But I do not make such superficial judgements. I consider your delicately pointed nose, and regard you as a genius on vacation.' I was annoyed by his embarrassing way of speaking, and I wanted to put him right, but he did not allow me to speak. 'Don't you see?' he said. 'You've already swelled up, just with this little bit of praise. Look inside yourself, and consider how dangerous this vocation is! We geniuses – for I am one also – care as little for the world as the world cares for us. In our seven-league boots – which in the near future prodigies such as ourselves will be born with – we stride unceremoniously on into eternity. Oh, what a very pitiable, uncomfortable position we are in, with one leg in the future and its hope of a new dawn and new life, and with the other leg still in the middle of Rome in the Piazza del Popolo where the children of this world seize the opportunity to hitch their wagons to our star and hang onto our boots until they almost pull our legs out of them. And all this tugging, wine-drinking and starvation merely for the sake of immortality! And look at my colleague on the bench there, who is likewise a genius. Time already seems too long for him, so what will he do in eternity? Yes, my highly esteemed colleague, you and I and the sun, we all rose early together this morning, and we have brooded and painted the whole day, and everything was fine. Now drowsy night is travelling through the world and wiping out all the colours with her fur sleeve.' He went on speaking. His hair was dishevelled with all the dancing and drinking, and in the moonlight he looked deathly pale.

But I had for some time had a horror of him and his wild talk, and when he turned round towards the sleeping painter, I seized the opportunity to creep unnoticed round the table and out of the garden. I climbed, alone and light-hearted, down past the vine trellises into the wide valley which was shining in the moonlight.

I could hear the clocks striking ten in the city. Behind me I occasionally heard the sound of a guitar and in the distance the voices of the two painters, who were now going home too. I ran on as fast as I could so that they could not ask me any more questions.

At the gate I turned right into the street, and rushed on with a beating heart between the silent houses and gardens. How surprised I was to see myself suddenly coming out into the square with the fountain, which I had not been able to find earlier in the daylight. There was the same lonely summer-house in the bright moonlight, and also the same beautiful lady singing the same Italian song as the evening before. In my delight I ran first to the small door, then to the main door of the house, and then with all my strength to the big garden gate, but they were all locked. Then it occurred to me that it had not yet struck eleven. I was vexed by the long time I had to wait, but good manners forbade that I should climb over the garden gate as I had done the day before. So I walked up and down for a while in the lonely square, and then sat down again by the stone fountain, full of thought and calm anticipation.

The stars were twinkling in the sky, the square was completely still and deserted, I was listening contentedly to the beautiful lady's song, which came to me through the murmuring of the fountain. Then I suddenly saw a white figure coming directly from the other side of the square up to the little garden gate. In the uncertain light of the moon I saw that it was the crazy painter in his white cloak. He took out a key, opened the gate, and before I knew what was happening he was in the garden.

I had already been nettled by the painter and his irrational speech, and now I was beside myself with anger. The dissolute genius is no doubt drunk again, I thought. He must have got the key from the chambermaid, and now he intends to creep up to the gracious lady, betray her, and attack her. And so I rushed through the little gate, which he had left open, and into the garden.

When I entered all was lonely and still. The folding door of the summer-house stood open, and a milky white ray of light came from it and played on the grass and the flowers in front of the door. From a distance I looked inside. There, in a splendid green room, dimly lit by only one white lamp, lay the beautiful lady on a silken ottoman, with the guitar in her hands, quite unaware in her innocence of the danger outside.

I did not look very long, however, for just then I saw the figure in white come from the other side of the garden and steal cautiously behind the bushes and up to the summer-house. The beautiful lady was singing so mournfully that it pierced me through and through. I did not hesitate. I broke off a hefty branch, ran with it straight towards the white cloak, and shouted out 'Murder! Murder!' at the top of my lungs so that the whole garden shook. The painter, when he saw me run towards him so unexpectedly, took to his heels with a horrible scream. I screamed even louder than he did. He ran to the house and I ran after him. I was about to grab him when I got caught up in the blessed flower-beds and I measured my length outside the door of the house.

'Oh, it's you, is it? You idiot!' I heard someone shout out above me. 'You frightened me to death!' I picked myself up, wiping the sand and soil out of my eyes. The chambermaid was standing there. The white cloak had fallen off her shoulders with her last stride. I was now completely at a loss. 'But wasn't the painter here?' I asked. 'Yes, of course,' she said in her saucy way. 'Or at least his cloak was. He put it round my shoulders when I met him at the gate. I was freezing.' While we were chattering the beautiful lady had got up from her ottoman and come to the door. My heart was thumping fit to burst. But I was amazed to see, when I looked in, that it was not my lovely lady, but someone utterly different!

She was a tall, rather corpulent, imposing lady with a proud, hooked nose and high-arched eyebrows – beautiful in a rather frightening way. She looked at me so majestically with her large sparkling eyes that I was overawed. I did not know what to do. I went on bowing to her in my confusion, and finally I tried to kiss her hand. But she snatched it away hastily, and said something to the chambermaid in Italian, of which I understood nothing.

Meanwhile the shouting had roused the whole neighbourhood. Dogs were barking, children screaming, and in between could be heard the sound of men's voices coming nearer and nearer to the garden. The lady gave me one more glance, looking daggers at me, turned back quickly into the room with a proud but rather forced laugh, and slammed the door in my face. But the chambermaid without more ado seized me by the arm and dragged me to the garden gate.

'You've done something stupid once again,' she said to me angrily, as we went. Now it was my turn to be angry. 'Hang it all!' I said. 'Didn't you tell me to come here yourself?' 'That's just the point,' cried the chambermaid. 'My mistress has been so kind to you, throwing flowers out of the window to you, singing arias – and this is all the thanks she gets for it! There's nothing to be done with you. You spit on your own good luck.' 'But I meant the German countess, my beautiful lady –' 'Oh,' she interrupted, 'she's been back in Germany a long time, together with your grand passion. You'd do well to get back there yourself! She is no doubt pining for you, and you could play your fiddle, and the two of you could gaze at the moon together – just so long as I don't set eyes on you ever again!'

But now there rose a hideous noise behind us. There were men with clubs in their hands climbing over the fence of the next garden, there were others cursing and searching all the paths, and desperate faces wearing nightcaps were peering over the hedges here and there in the moonlight. Altogether it was as though the Devil himself were hatching his whole brood out of the hedges and shrubbery. The chambermaid knew immediately what to do. 'There, there's the thief!' she shouted out, pointing to the other side of the garden. Then she shoved me out of the garden, and clapped the gate shut behind me.

So there I was once more, quite alone in the silent square,

just as I was when I arrived the previous day. The fountain, which had been glittering so brightly in the moonlight, as though angels were climbing up and down its spraying waters, was still playing indeed, but for me it was as though all my joy had been drowned in the water or gone up in smoke. I firmly resolved to turn my back for ever on the treacherous land of Italy, with its crazy painters, its oranges and its chambermaids. And that same hour I went out through the gate of the city.

CHAPTER NINE

The mountains stand like sentries round:
'Who's coming at this early hour
From foreign parts across the moor?'
I look where all the mountains stand,
And in my jubilation shout
Right from the bottom of my heart,
Watchword and war cry both at once:
'Hail, Austria!'

And now I'm recognised by all,
Greeted by all the birds around
As is the custom in this land.
The Danube sparkles through the vale,
And from a distance Stephen's spire[8]
Is rising up to meet me here.
It's in my mind. I'll see it soon.
Hail, Austria!

I was standing on a high mountain, the first which gave a glimpse of Austria, waving my hat in joy and singing the last stanza, when all at once I heard behind me in the wood the magnificent sound of wind instruments. I swivelled round and saw three lads in long blue cloaks. One was playing the oboe, another the clarinet and the third, who was wearing an old tricorn on his head, the hunting horn. They were accompanying my singing, and the woods re-echoed with the sound. Not wishing to be left out, I took out my fiddle and played and sang along with them. Then they began to look thoughtfully at each other, the horn player stopped puffing out his cheeks and laid his horn by, and then gradually they all became quiet and looked at me. In amazement I stopped playing too and looked at them. 'We thought,' said the horn player at last, 'because you are wearing a frock-coat, that you were an Englishman travelling on foot, enjoying the beauties of nature, and so we hoped to earn a little to help us on our way. But it looks as though you are a musician too.' 'I am actually a toll-keeper,' I answered, 'and I have come straight from Rome. But, since there have been no takings for a long while, I have been playing my violin to get me by.' 'That doesn't bring in much nowadays,' said the horn player, walking back to the wood and fanning with his tricorn a small fire which they had lit there. 'If anything, wind instruments pay better,' he went on. 'Whenever we find some noble company sitting quietly at their midday meal, we come upon them unexpectedly in their vaulted porch and then all three of us start blowing away fit to burst. Then a servant comes out straightaway with money or food for us – anything to make us stop our noise. But won't you have some lunch with us, sir?'

The fire was blazing away, the morning air was sharp, and we all sat round on the grass. Two of the musicians took a small pot off the fire. In it there was coffee with the milk already added. They took some bread out of their pockets, and took turns to dunk the bread and drink from the pot. It was a pleasure to see them enjoying it so much. But the horn player said, 'I can't bear that black muck,' and he gave me half a round of bread and butter and also produced a bottle of wine. 'Would you like a swig?' I took a hefty swig, but had to put it down again quickly, for it tasted quite vinegary. 'It's local produce,' said the horn player. 'But perhaps being in Italy has spoiled your German taste.'

Then he rummaged around in his knapsack and finally brought out, amongst all kinds of rubbish, an old tattered map on which there was still a picture of the Emperor in all his state, with his sceptre in his right hand and the imperial orb in his left. He spread it out carefully on the ground and the others gathered round to deliberate over what route they should take.

'Our vacation will soon be over,' said one, 'so we must turn left as soon as we leave Linz. That will soon bring us to Prague.' 'Do you really mean that?' said the horn player. 'Who can you play to there? There's nothing there but woodland and charcoal-burners. Certainly no refined appreciation of art and no free bed and board.' 'Fiddlesticks!' said the other. 'I prefer the peasants. They know where the shoe pinches and they don't make so much fuss about the occasional wrong note.' 'You say that because you've no sense of honour,' retorted the horn player. 'I, on the other hand, agree with the Roman poet, and *odi profanum vulgus et arceo*, which means roughly "I despise the uninitiated mob and I keep them at a distance."' 'But there must be some churches on the way,' said the third man. 'So we'll be able to lodge with the priest.' 'Count me out!' said the horn player. 'Priests always provide short commons and long sermons. They say we should not lead such a useless existence, but rather pursue our studies, especially when they look at me and see a possible future cleric. No, no, *clericus clericum non decimat*. Clerics don't take tithes from each other. What are we bothering about anyway? The professors are still in Karlsbad, and they won't be very punctual.' 'Yes, but *distinguendum est inter et inter*,' answered the other. '*Quod licet Jovi, non licet bovi*. What's sauce for the goose is not necessarily sauce for the gander.'

I realised now that they were students from Prague, and I conceived a great respect for them, particularly since the Latin simply flowed out of their mouths. 'Are you, sir, also a man of letters?' the horn player asked me. I told him modestly that I had always had a great desire to study, but had never had the money. 'That doesn't make any difference,' said the horn player. 'We haven't any money, and we haven't any rich friends. Anyone with a head on his shoulders knows what to do. *Aurora musis amica*, morning is the best time to study, or, to put it bluntly, don't linger over your breakfast. But when the noontime bells ring out over the town from tower to tower and from mountain to mountain, and the schoolchildren burst with a great shout from the dark schoolrooms and swarm through the streets in the sunshine, then we take ourselves off to the Capuchin monastery, to Father Cook, and find a table laid ready for us, or if there isn't one laid, there is still a full bowl for each of us, so it's neither here nor there, and we eat and perfect our Latin at the same time. And so you see, this is how we keep up our studies. And when at last it's vacation time, and the others go to see their parents, some by coach and some on horseback, we wander through the streets with our instruments under our cloaks and out of the town. And the world is our oyster.'

I do not know why, but as he explained all this, it went right to my heart that such learned people should be so forsaken by the world. I thought about myself and how it was really no different for me and the tears came to my eyes. The horn player stared at me in amazement. 'It doesn't matter,' he continued. 'I wouldn't like to travel as they do, with horses and coffee and beds with fresh linen and nightcaps and bootjacks all ordered in advance. What we like to do is to go out in the early morning, with birds of passage flying high over our heads, and not know what chimney is smoking for us today, and have no idea what may happen during the day.' 'Yes,' said the other, 'and wherever we turn up and take out our instruments everyone enjoys it. When we come to some villa in the country at midday and strike up in the hall, then the maids dance outside, and the master and his family order the dining-room door to be left ajar, so that they can hear the music better, and through that opening there comes the rattle of plates and the smell of roast meat to greet the joyful sounds we make, and the young ladies at the dining-table crane their necks to look at the music-makers.' 'That's exactly it!' cried the horn player, with his eyes gleaming. 'Let the others go on revising their notes if they want to. But our learning comes from the great picture-book which the good Lord has opened up for us outside. Yes, believe me sir, it is people like us who are the right ones to preach to the peasants and strike the pulpit with our fists until the clodhoppers down below feel their hearts bursting with edification and contrition.'

As they went on speaking, I felt so uplifted that I would have loved to study in their company. They could not talk too much for me. I like to converse with educated people because there is always something to learn from them. Unfortunately we did not get round to a rational discussion, since one of the students had been worried for a while that their vacation was coming to an end. He had therefore put his clarinet hastily together and propped a sheet of music on his knee and was practising a difficult passage from a Mass which he had to play with the others when they returned to Prague. So he sat there and fingered and blew, and played so many wrong notes that it set my teeth on edge and made it difficult for anyone to catch even his own words.

Suddenly the horn player exclaimed in his bass voice, 'That's it! I've got it!' He thumped the map which lay by his side. The other made a pause in his puffing and blowing and looked at him in surprise. 'Listen,' said the horn player. 'Not far from Vienna there is a palace, that palace has a major-domo, and that major-domo is my cousin! My dear fellow-students, we must go there and pay our respects to my cousin, and he will look after us and help us on our way.' When I heard this, I started up. 'He plays the bassoon, doesn't he?' I cried. 'And he's a tall, upright man with a large aristocratic nose?' The horn player nodded in agreement. In my joy I embraced him so fervently that his tricorn fell off his head. Then we all agreed straightaway to take the mail-boat down the Danube to the beautiful countess' palace.

When we came to the river bank, everything was ready for departure. The fat landlord, by whose inn the boat had been moored overnight, was standing expansively and comfortably in the inn door, which he filled completely, chatting and joking with those who were leaving, while from every window girls were waving to the sailors who were carrying the last packages on board. An elderly gentleman wearing a grey overcoat and a black cravat, who was about to travel on the boat also, was standing on the bank and talking earnestly to a young slim little fellow dressed in long leather trousers and a tight scarlet jacket, and mounted on a splendid English hunter. I was very surprised to see that they seemed to be looking at me every now and then and talking about me. Finally the old gentleman laughed, and the slim young fellow cracked his whip, galloped off as though he were trying to race the larks in the sky above, and disappeared into the landscape sparkling in the morning sun.

Meanwhile the students and I had pooled our money. The boatman laughed and shook his head in amusement as the horn player counted out our fare which was entirely in coppers. In our great need we had scraped it together by emptying all our pockets. But I jumped for joy to see the Danube before me once more. We sprang onto the boat, the boatman gave the signal and we sailed away between mountains and vineyards in the morning brightness.

Birds were singing in the woods, on all sides we could hear the village bells in the distance, and larks were warbling high in the sky. On the boat there was a canary which chirruped so that it was a delight to hear.

This canary belonged to a pretty young girl who was one of our fellow-travellers. She kept the cage close by her and had a tiny bundle of clothes under her arm. She sat quietly and contentedly by herself, looking sometimes at the new travelling shoes which peeped out from beneath her skirt, and sometimes down into the water below. The morning sun was shining on her pale forehead and on her neatly parted hair. I noticed that the students would have liked to engage her in polite conversation, for they kept walking past her, and the horn player kept clearing his throat and pulling now at his cravat and now at his tricorn. But they could not pluck up their courage, and the girl cast her eyes down whenever they came near.

Most of their embarrassment however was owing to the presence of the elderly gentleman in the grey overcoat, who was sitting on the other side of the boat, and whom they took for a priest. He was reading a breviary, from which however he often looked up to gaze at the beautiful countryside. The gilt edges of his book and the brightly coloured pictures of saints in it glittered in the morning sunlight. At the same time, he saw what was happening on the boat and he could tell a bird by its feathers. It was not long before he was speaking to one of the students in Latin, upon which all three of them approached him, took off their hats to him and answered him in Latin.

Meanwhile I had sat down in the bows of the boat,

contentedly letting my legs dangle down into the water, and always looking, as the boat ploughed on through the foaming waves, into the blue distance, and noticing how on the green banks one tower and one palace after another grew bigger and bigger and then disappeared behind us. If only I had wings today, I thought, and in my impatience I took out my fiddle and played all my oldest pieces through, those which I had learned when I was still at home and when I was in the palace of my beautiful lady.

Suddenly someone clapped me on the shoulder. It was the reverend gentleman, who had put his book away and had been listening to me playing for quite some time. 'Well, well, *ludi magister*, music master,' he said to me and he laughed, 'you are forgetting to eat and drink.' He told me to put my fiddle away and have a snack with him. He led me to nice little arbour which the sailors had erected out of young birches and firs in the middle of the boat. He had arranged for a table to be put there, and I, the students, and the young girl as well had to sit round it on barrels and packages.

The reverend gentleman now took out a large joint of meat and some slices of bread and butter, which had been carefully wrapped in paper. Out of a box he took several bottles of wine and a silver cup which was plated with gold inside. He poured out some wine, tasted it, caught the bouquet, tasted it again, and then handed it round to each of us. The students all sat bolt upright on their barrels and ate and drank very little, because of their great respect for their host. The girl too only touched her lips to the cup, glancing timidly at me and at the students. But the more often she looked at us, the bolder she became.

Eventually she told the reverend gentleman that she was going into service away from home for the first time, and was on her way to the palace where her new mistress was. At this I blushed all over, for she had named my beautiful lady's palace. She must be my future chambermaid, I thought. I felt dizzy. 'There's going to be a big wedding at the palace soon,' said the reverend gentleman. 'Yes,' said the girl, who would have liked to learn more about it. 'They say it is an old secret love, which the countess refused to permit.' The reverend gentleman replied only by saying, 'Hm, hm,' and filled his hunter's cup with wine and sipped it with a thoughtful look on his face. But I leaned right across the table, supporting myself on both arms, to make sure I missed nothing of the conversation. The reverend gentleman noticed this. 'I can tell you,' he went on, 'that the two countesses have sent me to find out whether the future bridegroom has already arrived here, for a lady has written from Rome to say that he left there a long time ago.' When he mentioned the lady in Rome I went red again. 'Are you then acquainted with the bridegroom?' I asked in my confusion. 'No,' replied the old gentleman, 'but he must be a bit of a card, a rather strange bird.' 'Oh yes, he is,' I said hurriedly, 'a bird who escapes from all the cages they put him in as soon as he can and sings happily whenever he finds himself at liberty once more.' 'And loafs around in foreign parts,' the gentleman continued calmly, 'goes about slowly by night and sleeps in front of people's doors by day.' That made me very annoyed. 'Sir,' I cried out excitedly, 'you have been misinformed. The bridegroom is a slim, moral, promising young man, whose time in Italy was spent in great style in an old castle, who has associated with no one but countesses, famous painters, and chambermaids, who knows how to look after his money, or would do if he had any, and who –' 'Well, well, I didn't realise that you knew him so well,' interrupted the reverend gentleman, and laughed so heartily that he went quite blue in the face and the tears rolled down his cheeks. 'But I heard,' the girl put in, 'that he was a tall gentleman, and very very wealthy.' 'Oh my goodness, yes, yes! Confusion, nothing but confusion!' cried the reverend gentleman, still unable to contain himself for laughter, until finally he burst out coughing. When he had pulled himself together a little, he raised his cup and said, 'Here's to the happy couple!' I did not know what to make of the reverend gentleman and his words, but I was too ashamed, on account of those doings in Rome, to tell him here in front of everyone that I myself was the lost happy bridegroom.

The cup travelled round rapidly, and the reverend gentleman spoke to everyone in a very friendly way, so that they all came to like him, and soon they were all talking happily with each other. Even the students became more and more talkative, and they told of their journeys in the mountains, and finally took up their instruments and started to play. The cool river air came in through the branches of the arbour, the evening sun was already gilding the woods and valleys as they slipped quickly past us and the river-banks re-echoed to the sound of the horn. As the music played the reverend gentleman became more and more cheerful, and he told some jolly stories about his own youth. He told how he too had travelled across hills and valleys in his vacations and had often been hungry and thirsty, but always happy, and how in fact all of a student's life was one long vacation, coming as it did between the dreary, restricted life in school and the seriousness of one's professional work. The students all drank up once more and struck up a fresh song which echoed far into the mountains:

The birds are flying southwards,
Making for sunnier climes,
And travellers are waving
Their hats in the morning beams.
They are the wandering scholars.
Out of the gate they stray,
And as they go they're playing
To sound their last goodbye.
O Prague, goodbye, goodbye,
We're wandering far away!
Et habeat bonam pacem,
Qui sedet post fornacem.[9]

At night we rove through the city.
Through windows far and wide
We see the people dancing
And dressed in all their pride.
We stand before the houses
And have a dreadful thirst,
Which comes from making music,
And playing fit to burst.
But after a little time
One brings a jug of wine.
Venit ex sua domo.
Beatus ille homo![10]

And now through all the woodland
We feel the north wind blow.
We wander over meadows
Wet from the rain and snow.
Our cloaks are streaming tatters,
Our shoes are long worn down,
But still we go on playing
And sing as we stride on:
Beatus ille homo
Qui sedet in sua domo
Et sedet post fornacem
Et habet bonam pacem![11]

All of us – the sailors, the girl and I – joined happily in the chorus every time, even though we knew no Latin. But I was happiest of all, for now I was just able to see my toll-house above the trees in the distance and the palace behind it in the evening sunlight.

CHAPTER TEN

The boat came to shore, and we all jumped onto the land, scattering in all directions, like birds when their cage is suddenly opened. The reverend gentleman said goodbye hurriedly and strode off towards the palace. The students, on the other hand, rushed off to a secluded thicket where they quickly beat the dust out of their cloaks, washed themselves in a stream nearby, and shaved each other. The new chambermaid, carrying her canary and her bundle of clothes, went to the inn at the foot of the hill. I had recommended this to her, because I knew the landlady would let her change her dress there before she presented herself at the palace. The beautiful evening went straight to my heart, and once they had all dispersed I did not hesitate but ran immediately to the palace gardens.

My toll-house, which I had to pass on my way, was still standing in the same place, the tall trees in the palace gardens were still rustling above it, and the yellowhammer, which always used to sing its evening song on the chestnut tree in front of the window, was still singing there, as though nothing had happened in the world in the meantime. The toll-house window was open, so I ran to it full of joy and looked in. There was no one in the room, but the clock on the wall was still ticking away gently, the writing-table still stood by the window, and the long pipe was in one corner as it used to be. I could not contain myself, but leapt in through the window and sat down at the writing-table in front of the big ledger. The green and gold sunshine still came through the chestnut tree, through the window, and onto the figures in the open book; the bees were buzzing about the open window and the yellowhammer on the tree outside was singing away all the time. But suddenly the door opened and a tall old toll-keeper, wearing my old dressing-gown with the spots on it, came in! Seeing me so unexpectedly, he stopped in the doorway, took his glasses off and glared at me furiously. I was startled too, and without a word I leapt up and ran out of the door and through the little garden, where I only just failed to trip over the blessed potato plants which the toll-keeper, on the advice of the major-domo, had replaced my flowers with. I heard him behind me coming outside and cursing me, but I was already sitting on top of the high garden wall and looking down into the palace gardens with a beating heart.

The scent of the flowers rose through the shimmering air amid the birds' rejoicing. The lawns and paths were all deserted, but the gilded tips of the trees nodded towards me, blown by the wind, as though they wished to welcome me, and through the branches at one side I could at times see the Danube twinkling to me.

Suddenly I heard singing in the gardens at some distance away:

Men's loud joy has gone to rest.
Earth is whispering as in dreams
Wonderfully through the trees
What the heart has hardly guessed:
All the grief of olden times
Strikes so gently that it seems
Summer lightning in my breast.

It seemed to me that both the voice and the song were known to me of old, as though I had heard them once in a dream. I thought and thought. Then, 'It's Guido!' I cried in delight, leaping down into the garden. It was the same song which he had sung that summer evening on the balcony of the Italian inn where I had last seen him.

He carried on singing, while I sprang over flower-beds and hedges towards the voice. As I was coming out between the last rose bushes I stopped as though spellbound. On the stretch of grass by the lake with its swans, glowing red in the evening sunlight, my beautiful lady was sitting on a bench. She wore a lovely dress and she had a garland of white and red roses in her black hair. Her eyes were lowered and, as she listened to the song, she was playing with her riding whip on the grass in front of her, just as she did once in the boat when I had had to sing the song about the beautiful lady. Opposite her sat another young lady, her smooth white neck covered with brown curls turned towards me, who was singing to her guitar as the swans swam round slowly in wide circles on the peaceful lake. Then the beautiful lady raised her eyes suddenly and screamed when she saw me. The other lady turned round quickly to look at me, so that her curls flew across her face, and when she recognised me she burst into uncontrollable laughter, jumped up from the bench and clapped her hands three times. At that instant a large band of little girls in short, lily-white dresses with green and red bows slipped out from among the rose bushes, so many that I could not imagine where they had all been hidden. They were holding a long garland of flowers, and they quickly formed a circle and danced round me singing:

We bring along the bridal wreath
With silk that's violet-blue.
We lead you to the festal dance
And the wedding banquet too.
A beautiful green bridal wreath
And silk that's violet-blue!

I recognised the song. It was from *Der Freischütz*. I recognised a few of the little singers too. They were girls from the village. I pinched their cheeks and would have liked to escape out of the circle, but the cheeky little creatures would not allow me to. I had no notion what this carry-on was all about, and I just stood there quite confused.

Then suddenly a young man dressed in elegant hunting clothes came out from behind the bushes. I could hardly believe my eyes, for it was Leonhard! The little girls opened their circle and then, as though bewitched, they remained standing utterly still on one leg, with the other stretched up, while they held the garland of flowers high above their heads with both hands. My beautiful lady was standing quite still, only looking over to me from time to time. But Leonhard took her by the hand, led her to me, and this is what he said:

'Love – all learned men agree on this point – is one of the most powerful qualities in the human heart. With one fiery glance love breaks down the bastions of rank and class. For love, the world is too narrow and eternity too short. Yes, it is indeed a poet's cloak which every dreamer in the world wraps round himself when he wishes to find refuge in Arcadia. And the further apart two separated lovers move from each other, the more does the travelling wind blow this glittering cloak about behind them in graceful swirls, and the bolder and more amazing become the folds of its drapery, and the longer and longer does the cloak become behind the lovers, so that a disinterested person cannot walk anywhere without stepping on it. Dear toll-keeper and bridegroom! Although you rustled along in this cloak to the banks of the Tiber, the little hand of her who is now your bride still held you fast by the end of your train, and however much you twitched and fiddled and blustered, you were still under the spell of her beautiful eyes.

And now that we've got to this point, you two dear, dear, foolish people, throw this blessed cloak about you, so that the rest of the world disappears from around you, and be as loving to each other as a pair of turtle-doves, and live happily ever after!'

Leonhard had hardly finished his sermon before the other young lady – the one who had been singing – came up to me, placed a crown of fresh myrtle on my head, and sang in a teasing manner, as she set the crown more firmly on my head with her face very close to mine:

> *Here's why I love you now,*
> *Here's why your head is crowned:*
> *The stroke of your fiddle-bow*
> *Struck me times out of mind.*

Then she stepped back a few paces. 'Don't you recognise the robbers who shook you out of the tree that time in the middle of the night?' she asked, curtseying to me and looking at me so charmingly that my heart leapt up. Then, without waiting for my answer, she started to walk round me. 'He really is the same as ever, with nothing Italian about him! But for heaven's sake, just look at his bulging pockets!' she cried out to my beautiful lady. 'Fiddle, clothes, razor, travelling bag, all mixed up together!' She kept turning me this way and that, and could not contain her laughter. My lovely lady had kept silent all this time, and in her modesty and confusion she did not dare to raise her eyes. It even seemed to me that at moments she was secretly annoyed by all the talking and joking. Finally she burst into tears, and hid her face in the other lady's breast. The latter at first looked at her in astonishment, and then pressed her to her heart.

But I was quite stupefied. For the more closely I looked at the foreign lady the more clearly I recognised her. She was none other than the young painter, Guido!

I did not know what to say and was going to ask for some explanation when Leonhard went to her and whispered something. 'Does he still not know?' I heard him ask. She shook her head. He thought for a moment. 'No, no,' he said finally, 'he must be told everything straightaway, or there will only be more confusion and gossip.' Then he turned to me and said, 'Toll-keeper, we haven't much time, so please be so good as to get all your amazement done with as quickly as possible. Otherwise your questions and wondering and headshaking afterwards may stir up all the old confusion among people, and give rise to fresh inventions and conjectures.' As he said this he drew me deeper into the bushes while the young lady took up the riding whip, which my beautiful lady had put aside, and brandished it in the air. As she did this, her brown curls fell over her face, but I could still see that she was blushing crimson. 'Now,' continued Leonhard, 'although Fräulein Flora here is acting as though she knew nothing of this whole affair, she did once give her heart away on the spur of the moment. Thereupon another man comes along and with great prologues and trumpets and drums offers her his heart and wants hers in return. But her heart already belongs to someone else, and someone else's heart to her, and that someone does not want his heart back, and does not want to give hers back. So there is a great fuss and bother – but haven't you ever read a romantic novel?' I said I had not. 'Well anyway,' he continued, 'you have at least been taking part in one. There was in short such confusion over these hearts that someone – myself in fact – finally had to interfere. One warm summer night I leapt onto my horse, lifted the lady onto another horse, under the alias of a painter called Guido, and we made off to the south in order to hide her in one of my lonely castles in Italy until all the hue and cry over hearts had died down. Meanwhile they had picked up our scent and from the balcony of the Italian inn, where you showed what a good sentry you were by falling asleep, Flora caught sight of our pursuer.' 'And so the hunchback –?' '– was a spy. We went off into the woods in secret, and left you to travel on alone along the route which had already been fixed. This deceived our pursuers and, what is more, it deceived my servants in the castle on the mountain, who were hourly expecting Flora in disguise and so, with more zeal than sagacity, took you for her. Even here in the palace people thought that Flora was living up in the castle. They made enquiries, and then they wrote to her – didn't you get the letter?' At these words I drew the note from my pocket in a flash. 'This letter?' I asked. 'It's for me,' said Flora, who up to now had not seemed to be paying any attention to our conversation. She snatched the note out of my hand, read it through and placed it in her bosom. 'And now,' said Leonhard, 'we must hurry to the palace where everyone is waiting for us. Yes, to the palace, as a matter of course, and as one expects of a well-bred novel. We have had discovery, remorse, and reconciliation. Now we are all happily together once more, and the day after tomorrow is the wedding.'

As he spoke a furious noise of kettledrums and trumpets, horns and trombones, came from the bushes all of a sudden. Cannons were fired and there was much cheering. The little girls started to dance again and heads popped out of the bushes, one above the other, as though they were sprouting from the ground. In all the bustle and turmoil I leapt from one side to the other, and in the growing darkness I gradually recognised one by one all the old familiar faces. The old gardener was beating the drums, the students from Prague in their long cloaks were playing there, and near them was the major-domo fingering his bassoon like mad. When I saw him there so unexpectedly I ran over to him and embraced him so violently that he got out of time with the music. 'Now really,' he cried to the students, 'he may travel to the ends of the earth, but he's still a buffoon!' And he played even more furiously.

Meanwhile my beautiful lady had secretly escaped from all this noise and she was running across the grass and out into the gardens like a frightened deer. I noticed this just in time and I ran after her. The musicians were fully occupied and saw nothing of this. Later on, when they did notice, they presumed we had gone to the palace, and the whole crowd of them marched off towards it still playing loudly.

But the two of us came at the same time to a summer-house. It stood where the gardens sloped towards the broad deep valley which was visible through its open window. The sun had already gone down behind the mountains, although a reddish vapour still shimmered in the warm evening as the music died away, and the quieter it was, the clearer was the murmuring of the Danube. I gazed at the beautiful countess, who stood before me flushed with running, and I could hear the beating of her heart. But I did not know what I could respectfully say to her, now that I so suddenly found myself alone with her. Eventually I took my courage in both hands, and her hand in one of them. She drew me to her and fell about my neck and I held her tightly in my arms.

She quickly tore herself away and in her confusion ran to the window to cool her glowing cheeks in the evening air. 'Oh,' I cried, 'my heart is bursting, I can't think straight, and it's just as though it's all a dream!' 'It's the same with me,' said my beautiful lady. Then after a while she continued, 'When I came back from Rome last summer with the countess, and we had been lucky enough to find Flora and had brought her back with us, but had heard nothing of you either here or there, I never thought that things would turn out like this. For it was only at midday today that the jockey – that nimble lad on the English hunter – came to the palace and told us breathlessly that you were on the mail-boat.' Then she laughed quietly to herself. 'Do you recall,' she asked, 'the last time you saw me, on the balcony? That was on an evening like this – calm, and with music in the gardens.' 'Who has died then?' I asked quickly. 'I don't understand,' she said, looking at me in amazement. 'Your ladyship's husband,' I replied, 'who was standing with you on the balcony.' She blushed. 'What peculiar ideas you do have!' she cried. 'That was the countess' son who had just come back from his travels. Since it happened to be my birthday, he led me with him onto the balcony, so that I could be cheered also. But is that why you ran away?' 'It was indeed!' I cried, and struck my forehead with my hand. But she shook her head and laughed out loud.

I was so delighted to have her chattering so happily and intimately with me that I could have gone on listening till morning. I reached into my pocket and took out a handful of almonds in their shells which I had brought with me from Italy. She took a few of them and we cracked them and stood looking contentedly out over the countryside. 'Can you see,' she said after a little while, 'that white villa over there, gleaming in the moonlight, which the count has given to us to live in, together with the garden and the vineyards? He has known for a long while that we are fond of each other, and he is very well-disposed towards you, for if he hadn't had you with him when he carried off Flora and escaped with her from the inn, they would both have been caught before they could be reconciled with the old countess, and everything would have turned out differently.'

'O my most beautiful, most gracious countess,' I cried, 'I am out of my mind with all these unexpected pieces of news! And so Leonhard –' 'Yes, yes,' she interrupted, 'that's what he calls himself in Italy. Those estates there belong to him, and he is now about to marry the beautiful Flora, our countess' daughter. But why do you call me countess?' I stared at her in astonishment. 'I am no countess,' she went on. 'Our gracious countess took me into the palace when I was brought here by my uncle, the major-domo, as a poor little orphan.'

Then I really felt as if a weight had been taken off my mind. 'God bless the major-domo for being our uncle! I've always had a high opinion of him.' 'He means well by you too,' she replied, 'if you would only behave with rather more decorum, he always says. You must wear more elegant clothes now.' 'Oh yes,' I cried in my joy, 'an English frock-coat, a straw hat, knickerbockers and spurs! And straight after our wedding we'll go away to Italy, to Rome, where the marvellous fountains play, and we'll take the students from Prague with us, and the major-domo!' She smiled and gazed at me affectionately. Music could still be heard in the distance, and fireworks were shooting up from the palace and across the gardens in the stillness of the night, and we could hear the Danube rippling below us – and everything was as it ought to be!

NOTES

1. This is a friendly joke at the expense of Eichendorff's friends, Achim von Arnim and Clemens Brentano, who had published what became the most famous collection of folk-songs in Germany, *Des Knaben Wunderhorn* (The Boy's Magic Horn).

2. A spoon was sometimes placed inside the cheek of a man being shaved, in order to stretch the skin.

3. How handsome he is!

4. Poor little thing!

5. A very good night to you!

6. 'God', 'heart', 'love' and 'frenzy'. The words suggest a declaration of love.

7. Scoundrel!

8. St Stephen's is the cathedral of Vienna.

9. Peace to him who sits by his own fireside!

10. He comes out of his house. Blessed is that man!

11. Blessed is that man who sits at home peacefully by his own fireside!

BIOGRAPHICAL NOTE

German lyric poet and novelist, Joseph Karl Benedikt Freiherr von Eichendorff, was born in March 1788. He was a Silesian nobleman by birth, living much of his early life on his parents' estate, Schloss Lubowitz. Eichendorff, alongside his older brother, William, studied law at the universities of Halle, Heidelberg, and Berlin, and his first extant poems date from 1804, the year before his matriculation at Halle. Early military zeal saw him abandon study for the Prussian War of Liberation (1813) against Napoleon, and again obey a call to arms in 1815. In October 1814 he had married Luise von Larisch. After university, Eichendorff wrote a novel, entitled *Future and Present* (1815), a work composed in Lubowitz and Vienna, where he studied to enter the Prussian civil service. He later worked as a government official from 1816–44, initially as a junior lawyer in Breslau, and then as a government adviser.

A devout Catholic, Eichendorff wrote to honour Nature, which he deemed to exist wherever God's work was untarnished by humanity. His poems have inspired composers such as Mendelssohn and Richard Strauss, and his songs are now as popular as *Volkslieder* (folk-songs). A master of the short story, and a versatile dramatist, Eichendorff also translated Calderón's religious dramas, and devoted his later years to a history of German literature. His most famous work, however, remains his novella of 1826, *Life of a Good-for-nothing*, which is considered a perfect example of Romantic narrative fiction. He died in 1857.

J.G. Nichols is a poet and translator. His published translations include the poems of Guido Gozzano (for which he was awarded the John Florio prize), Gabriele D'Annunzio, Giacomo Leopardi, and Petrarch (for which he won the Monselice Prize).

HESPERUS PRESS – 100 PAGES

Hesperus Press, as suggested by the Latin motto, is committed to bringing near what is far – far both in space and time. Works written by the greatest authors, and unjustly neglected or simply little known in the English-speaking world, are made accessible through new translations and a completely fresh editorial approach. Through these short classic works, each little more than 100 pages in length, the reader will be introduced to the greatest writers from all times and all cultures.

For more information on Hesperus Press, please visit our website: **www.hesperuspress.com**

To place an order, please contact:
Grantham Book Services
Isaac Newton Way
Alma Park Industrial Estate
Grantham
Lincolnshire NG31 9SD
Tel: +44 (0) 1476 541080
Fax: +44 (0) 1476 541061
Email: orders@gbs.tbs-ltd.co.uk

SELECTED TITLES FROM HESPERUS PRESS

Gustave Flaubert *Memoirs of a Madman*

Alexander Pope *Scriblerus*

Ugo Foscolo *Last Letters of Jacopo Ortis*

Anton Chekhov *The Story of a Nobody*

Mark Twain *The Diary of Adam and Eve*

Giovanni Boccaccio *Life of Dante*

Victor Hugo *The Last Day of a Condemned Man*

Joseph Conrad *Heart of Darkness*

Edgar Allan Poe *Eureka*

Emile Zola *For a Night of Love*

Daniel Defoe *The King of Pirates*

Giacomo Leopardi *Thoughts*

Nikolai Gogol *The Squabble*

Franz Kafka *Metamorphosis*

Herman Melville *The Enchanted Isles*

Leonardo da Vinci *Prophecies*

Charles Baudelaire *On Wine and Hashish*

William Makepeace Thackeray *Rebecca and Rowena*

Wilkie Collins *Who Killed Zebedee?*

Théophile Gautier *The Jinx*

Charles Dickens *The Haunted House*

Luigi Pirandello *Loveless Love*

Fyodor Dostoevsky *Poor People*

E.T.A. Hoffmann *Mademoiselle de Scudéri*

Henry James *In the Cage*

Francesco Petrarch *My Secret Book*

D.H. Lawrence *The Fox*

Percy Bysshe Shelley *Zastrozzi*